For what is a queen's garden but the king's own heart?
To nuture or neglect, as she sees fit.

Cari Lyn Jones

Lumina and the Goblin King

Lapis Moon Publishing

Lumina and the Goblin King

A fairytale by Cari Lyn Jones

Table of Contents

Just a bit of an introduction…

All over the world, stories are told of the Good Folk – fairies, goblins, spirits and the like. From all these tales there is one thing you are sure to learn; fairies are rarely flighty things that do no harm. They are wondrous and terrible… and they do not think as mortals do.

For some of you, the creatures you meet within these pages will be as old friends, for others, new ones. But whether old or new, it may be that introductions are in order. Because, like all storytellers, I have taken some liberties with the lore I found.

So, if while you're reading you find yourself wondering just *who* that goblin might be, or *why* this one is different than you remember (or if you are like me and just find such things interesting) turn to the pages in the back of the book. There you will find a little about goblins and fairies, and a bit about those curious things that fall in between.

And now, I hope you will enjoy reading *Lumina and the Goblin King*.

CHAPTER 1

Lumina Finds a
Silver Kitten

It was a golden morning, clear and bright. The tall grass hung heavy with dew, perfect droplets lining every petal and leaf so that they shimmered and flashed in the sun's light, as though the whole glade had been dusted with diamonds.

A figure flitted across this glowing tapestry. A curious sprite, no taller than a dandelion stalk. Her skin was honeyed-cream, and her hair as blue as lapis. The eyes through which she saw the world were the warmest gold, shining like the sun through amber. She wore a coat of moth wings overtop a dress of gossamer.

Dancing from leaf to petal to stem and back again, her tiny feet splashed through the dewdrops like a child through puddles. Her toes were deliciously cold, but the May sun on her face was warm.

She ran along the edge of a spider's web which brought her to a wild rose growing in the shadow of a lone pine tree. Its blossoms were the color of raspberries, their fragrance delicate and sweet, and its arching canes made twisted pathways, along which she danced on feet as light as thistledown.

A flash of silver caught her eye; a small paw, just visible in the gloom beneath the rose. She gently stroked the leaf closest to her and asked the rose to shift its canes, so that she might see more clearly what was hiding in its thorny shadow.

There, in the dirt and leaf litter, was a tiny silver kitten. It lay unmoving, its fur filthy and wet.

Poor thing, she thought, *to die all alone so far from your mother's warmth.*

In her heart stirred a strange sadness. It was a feeling she had never experienced before. She leapt down from her perch, going over to the small, pathetic body. She touched the pink nose. It was as big as her hand. Even as young as it had probably been, it would have stood almost as tall as she. Her chest felt heavy, the feeling of sadness growing till her heart was near to overflowing with it.

Then, unexpectedly, she felt a small puff of air against her hand and heard the softest mew. Startled, she leapt away, only to rush straight back to the kitten's side. She gently stroked the fouled fur, crooning softly. It was terribly thin and much more wet than the morning's dew could account for.

The sprite laid her cheek against the top of the kitten's head. The sense of sadness that had filled her heart was gone, replaced by another emotion for which she had no name.

"I will get you warm and dry," she promised as she gently stroked the fuzzy ear. "Just wait a little longer." With a final caress she left.

As she was leaving, she asked the rose to open its branches a little further so that the sun might shine down on the silver kitten, offering her thanks when it did so. Stepping out from beneath the shelter of the rose, she looked around. Having made her promise, she now found she was unsure how to fulfill it.

She walked along a row of mossy stones, until she came to a large boulder. Growing from a cleft near its top was a Rowan tree. There, amongst its snowy blossoms sat the Rowan Maiden combing her long hair, now pale green with the spring.

"Hello little sister," she called down to the sprite. "You seem unhappy."

"No sweet Rowan, I am not unhappy, but I do need help," the sprite answered. "I found a small kitten beneath the wild rose. But I am afraid he won't last through the night if I cannot find a way to get him dry and fed."

"Do not fret Lumina, such is the way of things. The warm earth will hold him in her embrace, and his little body will enrich the soil." The Rowan Maiden paused. "But I can see you do not wish this. Climb up; I will call my birds and we will see if any can help." The Rowan tree softly rustled its leaves, whispering a summons on the wind.

In no time at all, birds of all kinds had answered the Rowan's call. They flitted along its branches, calling back and forth to each other in curiosity. Lumina told them what she had need of, although not why. In a flurry of wings, they flew off in search of the soft materials she had asked for; things such as they would line their nests with.

Lumina thanked the Rowan Maiden, promising to return to tell her all that happened. Though she guessed the birds themselves would tell the Maiden all there was to tell, and far quicker than she. Hopeful that their search would be successful, she headed back to the wild rose to wait for their arrival.

Before the morning grew much older, they returned. The air around the wild rose was a riot with birds, their beaks and talons filled with soft grasses, or cattail fluff, or long fur shed from winter coats. But it was not until the magpies returned with laundry stolen from a farmer's clothesline that Lumina felt she had enough.

They dropped their burdens at the edge of the rose's shadow, then went to perch amongst the stems, curious as to the reason behind their labors.

Suddenly, a raucous cacophony of warning calls resounded through the glade.

"Cat!" chirped the little finches.

"Cat!" called one of the magpies. "Are we helping a *cat*?"

"Yes," said Lumina. "But he is very young,"

"He will grow!" they replied back.

"Then he will stalk us!"

"And pounce us!"

"*And eat us!*" the chorus proclaimed, their calls becoming even louder and more cacophonous.

"Peace!" Lumina cried, and the noise lessened, but did not silence all together. "While the kitten is here, he will bring no harm to you," she promised.

"Even when he is grown?" the birds asked.

"Even when he is grown," she assured them. Still the birds flitted around nervously, some calling warnings to their families further off. Lumina reached up to touch a leaf of the wild rose, sharing with it her desire, then turned once more to address the flock.

"You have done me a service, and in return I would give you a gift," said Lumina. At this the birds quieted, not wanting to miss the gift she would offer them.

"Each of you may take one small branch or leaf from this rose, but do not be greedy. Weave them into your nests, and no snakes will be able to steal into your homes to eat your eggs or young."

The birds seemed to think this was a fine idea. They chose small twigs which the rose relinquished readily to their beaks or talons, and rushed off to safeguard their nests and young.

Lumina carried in the birds' offerings by the armload, piling them beneath the canes in a little space the rose had cleared for her. She used her thorn knife to cut the cloth the magpies had brought into pieces as large as she could possibly manage to use. Then she began to dry and clean the kitten's fur as best she could.

It took a long time, but eventually the kitten was dry. The clothes she had used, now wet, were hanging from rose thorns everywhere. As for the unused clothes, grasses and such, she had gathered them up, making them into something of a nest where the kitten now lay. Overall it made something of a cozy den. She stood next to the kitten, running her fingers through his silver fur. Although he was warmer and drier, the kitten had still not opened his eyes.

"Are you thirsty, I wonder?" Lumina considered aloud. The silver kitten answered her with a weak mew, and she smiled. "I'll see what I can find."

Saying she would find something for him to drink turned out to be much easier than doing it. She found and discarded hundreds of half nut shells and old acorn caps until she came across an old turtle shell, whose occupant had long ago turned to dust. It was half again as long as she was tall, and she thought it would do as a saucer for the kitten. But how was she going to get water into it?

Pushing the turtle shell in front of her, she returned to look in on the kitten. She found him still curled up in his nest. Seeing him, a warm softness wrapped around her heart, and she wondered if it would always be like this. But help was what she needed now. So she climbed to the very top of the wild rose, and was surprised to see just how late it was. Twilight was already falling, washing the sky in dusky violet. The stars had not yet come out, but it would not be long before they showed their shining faces.

Just beyond the glade was a meadow where a small herd of deer grazed, as they often did at that time of day. Standing on the edge of the herd was a glorious stag.

"Swift!" Lumina called, her voice carrying out into the soft air.

The stag lifted his magnificent head, his ears twitching at her call. He ambled over towards her.

"Hello, my flower," he greeted her, nodding his head to her politely.

"Hello, my gallant," she replied, reaching out to stroke his antlered brow for a moment before her excitement got the better of her. "Come see what I have found!"

The rose obligingly moved some of its stems so that Swift could look down at the small creature sleeping in its shadow.

The stag cocked his head to the side. "A cat?" he asked.

"A kitten," Lumina corrected. "A beautiful silver kitten. I found him this morning, wet and filthy. I have dried him off, but I am sure he is thirsty. And so, to that end, I would ask a favor of you."

"Whatever you wish," he said, bowing his head to her once again. "If it is within my power to grant it."

"Thank you," she smiled at him, laying her tiny hand on his muzzle by way of thanks, before racing down the stems to where the turtle shell waited. She pulled it out to where Swift stood watching her.

"Could you carry this?" she asked, showing him the shell.

"I can," the stag said, though he sounded somewhat dubious. "But if you plan to fill it with water, I may not be able to."

"Oh," she replied, disheartened. This was all so new for her! If she was thirsty, she would drink dew from the leaves. If she was hungry, she would eat the nuts from the trees or the berries from the brambles. And even all of that was only for her pleasure, for she did not really need to eat or drink at all.

She ran her hand along the shell's edge, her head bowed. What was she to do now? The softness in her heart hardened until it was as immovable as a mountain.

"If I can find a way for you to carry it, will you?" she asked.

"Of course, my dear sprite," Swift assured her.

It was not an easy task, but she was determined. Soon, an abandoned bird's nest became a basket with the shell nestled safely inside it. A honeysuckle's tendrils made a pair of handles that she hoped would work.

Dusk had deepened into evening by the time she had finished. Swift had kept her company as she had gone about her task. Now that she was finished, he reached down to take the honeysuckle handles in his mouth, tipping his head slightly so that Lumina might easily sit on one of his antlers, which she did. With her arm wrapped securely around his brow tine, they set off.

He left the glade, and in a few bounding leaps had carried her across the meadow to the edge of a clear lake. He stood there for a moment, watchful as a stag should be, then set the bird's nest sling down on the sandy shore. Lumina slid from her perch, all the while looking at the shell and the water next to it and realizing another difficulty had arisen. How were they to get the water into the shell without it floating away, or the bird's nest falling apart?

True night was beginning to fall, and a feeling of

foreboding pressed down on her. She could think of nothing that she wanted more than to return to the kitten's side.

In the end, she decided to ask for help. She reached out with her foot and tapped the water's surface three times, calling out a name as she did so.

"*Serene?*"

She did not have to wait long for an answer.

From out of the water came a nixy, riding on the back of a giant golden snail. Her hair was the green of water weeds, and her skin was as lustrous as a pearl. Her face was as fair and fae as Lumina's, though her features were perhaps more delicate. She had on a dress made of fishes' scales, and from beneath its hem peeked a pair of frog's feet.

The snail came to rest on a lily pad, not far from the shore where Lumina stood.

"Lumina, and the gallant Swift, good evening to you both," the nixy said in her sweet, watery voice. She looked curiously at the shell and its sling sitting next to the water's edge. "What do you have there? Is it a boat?" she asked.

"Not a boat, sweet nixy, I've made it to carry water, not to float upon it," explained Lumina, her excitement causing her to forgo the usual courtesies she would have exchanged with the water sprite. "I found a kitten. He is thirsty, but too weak to walk so far. I had hoped that you could help me fill this shell with water so that Swift can bring it back to him."

"A kitten?" asked Serene, her face brightening. "Does he have soft fur, as silver as a moonbeam?"

"Yes," Lumina confirmed, albeit cautiously. The nixy's interest caused her excitement to ebb, anxiety blooming in its place. Water was always reluctant to let go of something it had once held, and would sometimes call it back to its embrace.

The nixy clapped her hands. "Oh, he was lovely!" she said. "He climbed from my water just the other day. I did so want to keep him but he very much wanted to leave, and he was trying so hard that I gave him a small push up onto the shore. I regret that a little, he was so beautiful," she said smiling wistfully. "But his brother and sisters are still with me. They had been in the water's embrace for too long and couldn't follow him," she sighed again. "Of course, I will help you."

The nixy leaned down from where she sat on the snail, dipping a finger into the water, she swirled it once then pointed to the shell. A tendril of water leapt from the lake to fill the shell up to the rim perfectly.

"I could not have asked for more," Lumina said sincerely, though a thread of worry still niggled at her heart. Then an idea came to her, a way for her to safeguard the kitten as well as show her gratitude.

"Would you accept a gift?" she asked the nixy.

"A gift? What sort of gift?" said the nixy, curiosity dancing in her eyes.

"A rose," answered Lumina, "a bright red rose, as red as a raspberry, with silver frosted petals. One that would bloom even in your garden beneath the waves."

The nixy's face shone with delight. "Oh, I love when the wind blows the rose petals to me! They smell so sweet and float like little boats. And it would bloom in my garden?"

"Yes, for as long as the kitten lives, your rose will bloom," Lumina promised her.

"It will be lovely! Come whenever you wish and I will help as I can," the nixy said as the snail carried her back down into the water.

Swift took up the honeysuckle handles of the shell's sling, Lumina seating herself once again amongst the stag's antlers. He stepped carefully out into the meadow, mindful of his burden.

Their return back to where the wild rose grew was much slower. Once there, he gently set his burden down on the ground, as close to the thorny canes as he could. Lumina slid down from her perch. Using the honeysuckle vine handles, she pulled the shell under the rose to where the kitten waited.

The kitten had shifted slightly while they had been gone, his paws now tucked tightly under him so that he looked like a tiny loaf of bread. Swift watched through the rose stems above as Lumina tried to coax the kitten to drink. She used a nutshell that she had discarded earlier to bring the kitten small amounts of water. He did not recognize what she offered him at first, but when he did, he drank greedily.

"Not so fast, little one! You will make yourself sick," said Swift, after Lumina's fifth trip back to the water.

"Will he? Well then, I guess that is enough water for now." said Lumina, stroking the kitten's pale fuzzy head.

"There will be more for you later, but now we have to feed you... what do I feed you?" She wondered aloud.

"I would say feed him what you would feed any baby, milk," said Swift. "I know of a farmhouse not too far away. I could take you there in the morning if you would like."

"Yes, thank you my gallant one," she said, as she laid her cheek against the top of the kitten's head. "Don't worry dearest, I will get you food soon."

The moon had set and Swift had long ago returned to his does. Lumina brought more water to the kitten. She had imbued it with the same vitality as she would have a seed she wanted to help grow, and hoped it would help him until she could bring him food.

For now she was tucked up alongside the kitten's head, surrounded by his soft fur. She hummed softly to him and he purred back at her until sleep claimed them both.

The next morning, Swift was waiting for her when she woke. The shadows still lay thick beneath the rose, and it would be sometime before the sun peaked her shining head over the horizon. It was a good time for them to set out. Lumina stroked the sleeping kitten's ear, promising him that she would return soon. As she left, she gently brushed the rose's leaves. The canes closed behind her, making a thorny wall that few would dare to challenge.

The stag stepped gracefully out from beneath the trees, into the pale light, with Lumina once again perched in his antlers. In one great leap they were off, the glade quickly falling behind them, and the meadow soon followed. When they reached the lake, Swift slowed, following the shore until they came to a broad, quiet stream which wandered away from the lake, leading them out across rolling downs.

The sun was fully in the sky when the roofs of the farmhouse came into view. Cautiously, Swift approached the tall hedgerow that surrounded the well-tended pastures. Once there he stopped.

"I am sorry my fawn, but I cannot go any closer," he said. "They have dogs and if they scent me they will set up a clamor, and that will do you no good."

Lumina stroked the edge of one sleek ear. "Don't fret dear one, this will be fine," she said. "I am just happy you could carry me so far."

"Do you want me to wait?" Swift asked, but Lumina knew that he worried at being gone from his family for so long.

"No," she replied. "Go back to your does and fawns. There is no need for you to stay."

The stag lowered his head, and she slid down from his antlers. Still he did not leave, reluctant to abandon her, but she waved him away with the promise that all would be well. She passed beneath the dark branches of the hedgerow, and out into the sunlit pastures that surrounded the farmhouse.

She met a friendly goat at the pasture's edge who was only too happy to give her a ride. Sitting between the

silky ears, she listened as the old nanny gossiped, telling her all about the farmer and farmwife, as well as the
milkmaid and the herdboy. Though most of her thoughts
were of the new billy, who she was afraid would not be
interested in an old goat like her.

The nanny goat carried Lumina all the way to where
the gate opened onto a path that led to the milking shed.
There the sprite left the nanny goat and followed the
path as it ran along the back of the farmhouse. Harebells
grew along its edge, and she stopped to gather a few; they
would make perfect satchels. Continuing on, she came
to the path's end where the milking shed stood. Up its
ivy covered wall she went, until she came to a sun-filled
window left open to the morning air. Lumina could see
the milkmaid, and the herdboy too, but she paid them no
mind. They were certainly paying none to her, or anything
else but each other, and how comfortable the hay in the
corner was.

There was no milk that she could see. But sitting there
on the table beneath the window, in a square of morning
sunlight, was a crock of goat cheese. Lumina slipped her
satchels from her shoulders and quickly filled each with a
large dollop of the creamy white cheese. Carefully folding
the petals closed, she asked them to hold tightly so the
cheese would stay in place for her long journey back home.

She slid down from the lip of the crock, ran up a sunbeam to the windowsill and was out across the garden
without the milkmaid or her beau any the wiser.

As she passed the farmhouse, the door opened and out
came the farmwife. The woman might have only seen a

swirl of dust and not the sprite who walked along her path, but Lumina saw her and what she picked up off the stoop.

It was a little wooden bowl with a small plate, and the sight of them sent a shiver over Lumina's skin. She was sure that only the night before the plate had held bread and honey and the bowl had been full of goat's milk. A tribute left by the farmwife for the goblins to take back to their king in return for his good will and protection. And that meant that she was certainly not welcome here.

When Lumina reached the pasture, the old nanny goat was kind enough to carry her back across to the hedgerow. Lumina left her a gift by way of thanks - a sprig of thyme knotted in the old goat's tail - and promised that the new billy would not be able to resist the nanny's charms.

Back under the hedgerow and through the tall grass she went, until she reached the edge of the quiet stream she and Swift had followed earlier. As luck would have it, a large piece of birch bark floated by before long, the water carrying it over to the bank where Lumina stood. She climbed aboard, thanking the stream for its kindness.

The birch boat sailed smoothly downstream on the crystalline water, as it gently flowed between its grassy banks, murmuring over large rounded pebbles that sparkled in the bright morning light.

Lumina looked down at the four harebell satchels that rested in the bottom of her boat. She was sure it would not be enough for her kitten. He would certainly need more than this to eat. She thought again of the bowl and plate that the farmwife had picked up. The fear she had felt was forgotten, an idea growing in its place. The enmity between the Fairy Queen and the Goblin King might be a long-standing one, but such matters had little to do with her. And besides, her kitten needed to eat. So, as she continued to drift down the lazy stream, she thought a great deal about the tribute that the farmwife would leave out that night for the goblins, and how it would help feed her kitten, but not at all of what consequences might come of it.

The stream eventually emptied out into the nixy's lake. There on the shore, as if he had been waiting for her, was Swift. He carried her and her bundles back to the wild rose which was quickly becoming home.

Even as Lumina's feet touched the ground, below which the furthest of the wild rose's roots grew, the great thorny wall it had woven of its canes began to unfurl. The kitten waited for her there, his pale blue-gray eyes peering out from beneath the toothy leaves. She went to him and rubbed his fuzzy ears, showing him what was in the harebell satchels she carried.

As she had suspected, it took very little time for the kitten to finish off the food that she had brought. Still Lumina could not keep the smile from her face as he sat cleaning his paws and then her hands.

They snuggled down together in the kitten's little nest and slept the rest of the morning away.

When she woke later that day, the only thought in her mind was how to go about bringing the milk back for her kitten. By the time the sun began to sink towards evening, she had a plan firmly in mind. But there were some things she had to attend to first if she was to keep her kitten warm and safe while she was gone.

She went to stand at the edge of the rose's shadow, and as dusk fell, she drew a tiny wooden box out from the spider-silk bag hanging at her hip. She opened it, and pulling out a pinch of ash, gently blew it into the air, softly breathing a name as she did.

"*Ember*," she called, her words carrying the ashes out onto the wind. "I have need of you."

She watched and waited, until out of the deepening gloom a glowing spark spun and danced towards her on the night wind. It floated past, settling on a pile of twigs she had gathered earlier just for that purpose.

From the spark grew a figure, unfolding itself until it stood taller than she did. His skin was as black as coal, and his eyes were a bright, burning gold. Flames wreathed his head instead of hair. He swayed slowly and sinuously as he moved from twig to twig. Everywhere he stepped, the wood began to smolder and burn beneath his feet.

"You called me, sweet one?" the salamander asked, never pausing in his dance.

Lumina sat down in the circle of light made by the fire, though she was careful not to sit too near the flames.

"Yes, Ember I do. I found a kitten who needs to be kept warm," she said. The salamander's gaze sharpened, and for a moment it seemed he saw her and the kitten clearly. Then his eyes became vague again, seeing a world she could not.

"I am at your service, as always," he said, sweeping her a graceful bow in one turn of his never-ending dance. "Will you dance with me?"

"I will," Lumina promised.

"And will you give me a strand of your hair, to renew our friendship?" he asked.

"Of course, but first I have to leave on an errand."

"Leave?" the salamander asked, his gaze focusing once again on where she sat. "Are you going far?"

"To a farmhouse, a little ways from here. They put a bowl of milk out every night and I hope to bring some back for the kitten," she explained.

"If they put a bowl of milk out every night, sweet one, then they are paying tribute to the goblins. And it is not wise for you to take it," Ember pointed out. There was no admonishment in what he said, but the flames around him died down slightly making her wonder if he worried.

"I know," she admitted, "and I considered that."

"Ah," said Ember. The flames at his feet barely flickered above the twigs, the steps of his dance now slow and cautious. "And what of the consequences if you are caught?"

"I don't know. But my kitten has to eat, and so I have to go," Lumina said.

"If you feel you must, then you must. But be careful." The salamander reached out towards where Lumina sat, but pulled his fingers back before he could touch her. "Set me a boundary sweet sprite, one of little white stones, so that I know where to burn and where not to.

I do not see the world as you do, and if no clear limit is set, you will come home only to find that you no longer have a home to come to."

CHAPTER 2

A Bowl of Milk and
Bread with Honey

The night was still young, the stars barely a glimmer in the dusky black sky when Swift brought her once again to the farmhouse.

He lowered his head, tilting his antlers so that Lumina could untie the turtle shell from them. She did not have the bird's nest sling this time. It would have been of no use given what she had planned.

"Be careful," Swift said, his large, lovely eyes watching her with concern.

"I will be," she promised, resting her hand on his nose. After a final caress, she turned to where the turtle shell sat rocking on its back. Flipping the shell over, she slipped underneath and began carrying it toward the farmhouse. She did not see Swift leave, but heard the sound of his hooves fade in the distance.

The shell was awkward to carry, being half again as long as she was tall, and even though the grass was kind enough not to impede her passing, her going was slow. She trudged along, peering out from under the shell's rim. She could see little shivers run through the grass around her. They were soon followed by small gusts of wind that swirled up to join her beneath the shell.

"What are you doing?" asked a voice, as low and whispery as a wind through pine boughs.

"Yes, what are you doing? Is it a game?" asked another, whose voice rang sweetly, like wind chimes.

"Can we play?" a third voice asked, deeper than all the rest.

Shapes formed around Lumina, clear as dew drops shimmering in the moonlight. Soon there were three sylphs peering intently at her, their faces full of curiosity. She told them about the silver kitten, deciding that no harm would come from it. But she did not tell them why she was carrying the old turtle shell through the long grass.

"Oh, I think Zephyr has seen him! Under the wild rose that grows near Old Father Pine," said the sylph with the whispery voice.

"Yes, I have!" the sweet-voiced sylph chimed in, swirling around excitedly. "I loved his fur," she admitted, "and his whiskers tickled."

Curiosity peaked, the three sylphs, whose names she learned were Mistral, Zephyr and Gale, joined her in carrying the shell, all the while peppering her with questions about the silver kitten.

But, it is hard to keep the wind in one place for long, so after a time she found herself once again alone in her task. Still, they had shortened her journey by quite a bit. So when the stone stoop of the farmhouse loomed up in front of her, it was early enough that lights still burned in some of the farmhouse windows.

She could see the bowl and plate on the stoop, just as she had hoped. But she would not go up to take them yet. Instead, finding a large clump of thyme, she hid beneath it to wait for the lights to go out. She hoped that the goblins would not come to collect the tribute left for them until after the midnight hour, when all would be asleep. And with luck, by then she would be far away from this place, floating down the stream with a shell full of milk towards the glade where her kitten was waiting.

The moon had risen by the time the lights finally went out in the house. The night was now filled with a velvety darkness. The midnight hour was still far away, and Lumina had seen no one while she waited. She decided the time had come.

She pushed the shell closer, until it was just beneath the edge of the stoop, which loomed high over her head. Once there, she flipped it over, leaving it to rock gently on its top like a boat stranded on land. She hurried over to a rosemary planted next to the door, who kindly bent its stems, making a pathway for her to run along until she reached the top of the stoop. Waiting on the corner just as it should be, was the milk and slice of bread left by the farmwife as tribute to the goblins. Her heart was light with the thought of finding food for the kitten as she hastened towards it.

A shape moved in the inky blackness that pooled in the doorway. As quick as thought, she wrapped herself in moonbeams and starlight, so that to anyone with eyes, it would appear as if she was only a single violet growing up from a crack in the stone.

From out of the gloom hopped an old toad, huge and somewhat glum-looking. Lumina laughed and unfolded herself from her glamour.

"Ah, grandfather toad, you startled me," she said, but the toad said nothing in return.

It occurred to her then, that goblins often rode on the backs of toads. She looked around but saw no one.

She continued on to where the bowl of milk sat, and peered over the edge of the stoop to where the shell waited below.

"The bowl will have to be moved over a bit before it is properly aligned," an ominous voice said from behind her.

Lumina turned. A figure coalesced from out of the night, towering over her in a coat made of shadows. The darkness conspired to hide his features, save for pinpricks of white fire that burned where his eyes should be. A looming nothingness surrounded him, a void whose black tendrils reached out hungrily to engulf her, as if she were a single flame it was intent on devouring.

"Were you truly going to take from us?" he asked in creeping whispers. "That is bold. Why, I wonder?"

Lumina could not answer him. All her words had fled, leaving only a sinking void in her stomach and a trembling in her limbs. Everything around her had disappeared. There was no moon; no stars; only his all-consuming darkness and sepulcher voice.

"And do you understand the price?"

In her mind she saw little silver paws and fuzzy ears, laying there all alone, a tiny wasted corpse. There was one price that she would not pay. The trembling in her limbs stopped and her words came back to her again.

"Whatever the debt, I will pay it," she said firmly and she did not flinch when she looked into the blazing white fire of his eyes. "There is a tiny kitten, too young to find his own food. He needs milk if he is to live, and I know of no other place to find it."

"And you want this kitten to live?" the goblin asked, his voice coming from nowhere, and everywhere.

"I do," Lumina replied.

"Enough to indebt yourself to us?" he asked, the flames of his eyes drawing her in like a moth to its doom. Still there was no hesitation when she answered.

"Yes."

"Indeed," he said, straightening once again to his full height. The darkness fell away, so that his features were clearly etched in the silver light of the moon, which she could see once again, shining in the heavens above.

The goblin before her was no less intimidating now that she could see his face. The upper part was that of a crow with obsidian feathers that flowed across his cheeks and over his head, falling down his neck past the collar of his coat. The sharp beak overshadowed a chin and jaw that were alabaster white and as well-shaped as any fairy man's. Even his eyes were like a crow's, save for the white fires burning in their depths.

The silence stretched out between them, but the goblin

made no other move, just stood quietly watching her. She did not know why he waited or what game he was playing, and truth be told, it mattered little to her at the moment. A hungry kitten awaited her return and that was foremost in her heart. Settling her resolve, she turned her back to the goblin man. He did not try to stop her when she took the bowl's rim firmly in hand, slowly tilting it until the milk it held spilled over the edge.

As soon as the first drop fell, he joined her. Grasping the rim, he helped pour the milk steadily into the waiting shell below. It occurred to her then why he had said nothing. It was not until she poured the milk that she had well and truly stolen it. And with that one action, she had made her choice. There was no doubt that she now owed a debt to the Goblin King.

Still, she could not feel anything but happy as she made her way down to where the shell waited below, now full of milk. Without hesitation, she began pushing it back the way she had come, but found the shell much heavier than it had been before. She realized the return journey would be much slower going; a fact that made her worry greatly. Hands joined hers on the rim of the shell, pale and scaled like a bird's, with each long finger tipped in a wicked black talon. She looked up at the goblin man standing next to her, grateful despite everything the future might bring.

"Won't there be trouble if you help me?" she asked.

"Quite possibly," he replied, looking down at her. "But what form that trouble will take remains to be seen."

He brought with him the piece of brown bread heavy with honey, balancing it on the rim between them. Without another word, he began to help her push the shell across the pasture towards the quiet stream.

The wind had returned and with it the sylphs, laughing gaily as they ruffled through the goblin's feathers, making a game of tugging at the hem of his great coat. He did not swat or admonish them, so they soon tired of their game and raced ahead. The grass left in their wake lay flat and smooth, making it easier to push the shell along. This made the journey to the stream much faster, a fact for which Lumina was grateful. The desire to return to the kitten pressed more and more heavily down upon her.

At the stream's grassy edge they stopped and Lumina turned towards her silent companion. The pockets of her moth-wing coat were filled with all manner of things; some precious, some not, but all had meaning to her and would therefore make appropriate gifts. From its depths she pulled a bauble; a tiny quartz sphere, as clear as a dewdrop, which fit perfectly in the palm of her hand.

"A gift, for your help," she said, holding the tiny jewel out towards the goblin man.

"You owe me no debt for helping push this to the stream," he told her. He did not look down at the bauble in her hand but instead stared steadily into her eyes. Once again she found she could not look away.

"All the same, I would give it to you," she said, wanting desperately to get back to her kitten and away from his bewitching eyes.

"Indebting yourself to the Goblin King is not a small thing," he said, not reaching for the gift she offered him.

"I am curious to meet this kitten whose survival means so much to you."

The tendril of the fear she had felt earlier coiled and writhed in her stomach. He meant to go with her? Once he saw him, would the goblin try to take the silver kitten from her? Would he bring him harm? No, she could not let that happen. In her heart, a war was silently taking place as she stood there with her hand outstretched, the gift she would give shining in her palm. Still the goblin did not move to take it, continuing to watch her with his unfathomable eyes.

The moment stretched on for an eternity before he finally asked.

"Do you fear me?"

She did not answer him, but instead proclaimed adamantly, "I will not let you take him, nor bring him any harm!"

"Take him? No, I have no desire to take him from you; in fact, if all you have said is true, you have no reason to fear me," he said. "Further, I will promise you this; I will visit no harm on you or yours as long as none is offered to me or mine."

He reached out, taking the bauble from her hand, his talons delicately scraping her skin as he did so. A warning should her words prove false.

"My oath on it," he said. "And so I am bound, by the sun and the moon, the wind and the rain and by my own true name."

It was a powerful oath, binding him to his promise with unbreakable chains. The very essence of who he was would be forfeit should he break his word. He bowed slightly to her.

"Now, will you take me to meet this wondrous kitten of yours?" he asked.

"Given an oath like that, how can I not?" she replied.

Together they slid the shell full of milk into the water. Sitting on their respective sides with the bread balanced between them, they floated down the sleepy stream, the moon and stars lighting their way.

The crystalline waters carried them far from the farmhouse, with its hedgerows and pastures. While they floated along, the goblin man asked her how she had come to be caretaker of a kitten.

So she told him about finding the tiny creature, wet and filthy, under the wild rose. How she had dried him off with the help of the Rowan Maiden and her birds. And of Swift's help in bringing water back to him. She told the goblin about how she had learned of the fates of the kitten's brothers and sisters and how it was him alone who had climbed out of the lake. And she could not just let him die, could she? Not after he had tried so hard to live.

And all the while the goblin sat quietly as she told her tale, sharing the brown bread he had brought from the farmhouse. It was sweet and delicious, and Lumina savored every bite as she extolled the kitten's many virtues as she saw them. Through it all he listened intently, only asking her a question here and there. She may have wondered at this had she not been caught up in recounting tales of tiny pink paws, little fuzzy ears, and soft fur the color of moonshadows.

So lost was she in the telling that she was taken by surprise when the stream's quiet waters emptied out into the nixy's lake, carrying the shell boat along with them.

The shore closest to the wild rose was still on the far side of the lake, waterlilies stretching far out in front of them. She brushed a finger along the edge of one lily pad, asking for their help. They kindly gave it, pushing the little boat along from one lily pad to the next until it reached an open stretch of water. There they were left to drift, but not for long.

Shimmering scales flashed just below the water's dark surface, as a school of silvery fish swirled beneath them, carrying the turtle shell boat towards the other shore. Atop of one of those sleek bodies sat Serene. Smiling, the nixy called out to Lumina, her greeting faltering only when she saw the tall dark form of Lumina's companion.

The goblin reached down towards one of the fish swimming alongside their boat. "For your mistress," he said, handing the last piece of bread to it. "A tithe to you, lady, for the passage," The goblin nodded his head politely towards Serene.

The fish dutifully brought the bread to her mistress. The nixy took it from the fish's mouth, and nibbled on it hesitantly.

"Mmmm, delightful!" She said, gobbling up the remainder.

Serene followed them across the whole of the lake, strangely silent, though whether that was because of shyness or wariness, Lumina could only guess. When they came to the other shore, Lumina reached into the small bag at her hip for the third time that night. She took from it a seed as big as her fist and handed it to Serene.

"My gift to you for your help, as promised," she said. "Its first leaves will appear by the new moon."

"It is beautiful," said the nixy, holding the rose seed gently in her hand. Her excitement set her face aglow as she disappeared beneath the surface of the lake, taking her charges with her.

Lumina was glad she had not given her gift to Serene sooner, since it was quite likely they would have been quickly forgotten and left to drift wherever the current would take them. As it was, they were still a ways from shore, and the moon now riding high in the sky was a reminder of just how late it was. The anxiousness that had all but disappeared as she told her companion about the kitten returned a hundredfold, and her heart fluttered in her chest.

"It is so late," she said aloud, her companion half-forgotten in her growing concern.

"Are you worried?" he asked, tilting his head slightly as birds will often do when spying something interesting.

"Yes," she answered, near choking on her desire to be back with her kitten, in the wild rose's protective embrace.

The goblin regarded her for a while longer, and then, his decision apparently made, called out a name.

"*Hoax.*"

He had not spoken loudly, but that single word resonated

out into the night, rippling through the air and down into the water, like the deep tolling of a bell.

All around them the surface of the lake began to shiver. Their boat shied and shifted beneath them, as two pointed ears rose up from the depths. The ears were soon followed by a pony's shaggy head, and before long a phooka was standing chest deep in the water beside them. His mane hung lank with waterweed and lilies. His hide was the same color as the space between the stars, but his eyes glowed green like marshlights.

"You called," the phooka answered, his voice full of laughter.

"I did," replied her companion. "I am in need of a favor."

"A favor? For you or this lovely sprite?" asked the phooka.

"For me," answered the goblin.

"Pity," said the phooka, "but as always, I am at your command. Tell me what you wish done and I will do it gladly."

"This shell needs to be carried to the edge of the glade over there, without spilling any of the milk it holds. Can you do that?" he asked the phooka, but the manner in which he asked made the answer seem a foregone conclusion.

"Of course," the phooka answered.

The phooka, Hoax (or at least that was who Lumina assumed him to be), lowered himself back down into the water until only his nostrils showed above the surface, filling Lumina's vision like great fluttering caves. Then he opened his mouth — impossibly wide it seemed —

and she was greeted with the sight of teeth, sharp and numerous and surely unlike ones any herbivore had ever possessed. Despite that, he scooped the boat up gently enough, rising very quickly out of the water.

As he did so, her companion took her by the hand, and led her up between the two quivering nostrils. Together they made their way to a spot between the phooka's small pointed ears. There she sat amidst the strands of his tangled forelock, while her companion stood just beside her, one hand resting on the edge of a furry ear. The phooka stepped smoothly out into the meadow, towards the quiet glade beyond.

It took no time at all for him to reach the place where the wild rose waited, its branches drawn so tightly together that barely a glimmer of firelight seeped through.

The phooka stopped, and stood a while, his ears flipping back and forth in consternation. The goblin beside her chuckled.

"I see that you did not think this through entirely," he said to the phooka who gave a small snort, but otherwise had nothing to say.

Being so close, Lumina found that she could not wait to see the kitten. Leaving the phooka to his dilemma, she stepped easily from her perch atop his head to one of the tallest of the wild rose's arching canes. Along the branches' twisting pathways she went, and at her touch, they began to rustle and unfurl. Ember still danced in the circle of white stones just as he had been when Lumina had left. He did not acknowledge her as she passed, but his dance slowed when she entered into his circle of light, which now spilled out into the darkness through the open branches.

When she reached the bottom, she found the kitten still curled up in his nest of wild thyme and cattail fluff.

"I'm back dearest," she said, stroking his fuzzy head. He purred weakly at her touch but did not open his eyes. "I have brought you milk, you need only be patient for a little while longer" she promised, before heading out to where she had left the goblins waiting on her doorstep.

When she came out from beneath the rose's sheltering branches, she was greeted by the strangest sight. The phooka was kneeling with his head at the most absurd angle, trying to slide the shell full of goat's milk from his mouth onto the ground without spilling even the tiniest bit. An act made much more difficult when one did not have thumbs.

The goblin man whom (given his appearance) she had come to think of as Crow, stood at the edge of the firelight, offering encouragement and insult in equal measure. Finally, the shell was safely on the ground, unsplit, and with barely a ripple on the milk's pale surface. With that accomplished, Hoax rose back up to his feet, shaking his mane, clearly pleased with himself.

"As always, your wisdom is the bright light that guides me," he said to the goblin, offering a small, respectful nod of his pony head, though Lumina would have been hard pressed to say whether it was sincerity or mockery that she heard in the phooka's voice.

Walking up, Crow laid a hand alongside one nostril. "You did well," he said; his sincerity, at least, was clear.

Even while Crow praised the phooka, Lumina began nudging the shell along. Once again the goblin joined her, and side by side, they pushed the shell into what had become her cozy den beneath the wild rose.

Seeing that the kitten's eyes were open now, she left the shell to go over to him. She stroked her hand along one ear, all the while crooning her reassurance to him. She heard the goblin coming up behind her.

At his approach, the kitten tried to stand, flattening his ears as he hissed softly at the stranger. Fearlessly, the goblin continued to walk up to him, laying his hand on the kitten's nose despite its warning growl.

"Peace," he said. "I mean no harm to you or your mistress."

At his voice the kitten stilled, his growl growing silent.

"There now," the goblin continued, his voice comforting, like a warm sunbeam on a winter morning. "Your mistress has brought you food which I can see you sorely need."

With that, he nudged the kitten the rest of the way to his feet and helped Lumina steady him as he wobbled to the shell full of milk.

Once there, the kitten needed no urging to begin lapping at the milk. Lumina watched, a smile blooming across her face. Her heart felt full and warm as a summer's day. She felt deliriously happy, which was not an uncommon feeling for her, but now she also felt something altogether new... pride.

"Isn't he beautiful!" she exclaimed, beaming her smile across the top of the kitten's head to where Crow stood on the other side. Her hand unconsciously reached out to stroke the silver fur again.

"He is," he agreed, reaching out his own hand to stroke the kitten. His obsidian talons scratched delicately behind the fuzzy ears. At this the kitten began to purr, a pleasant rumble that did not interrupt his meal in the slightest.

It took very little time until the kitten had drunk his fill. His tummy round and full, he lay sleeping, flopped in a boneless heap that only the very young can achieve.

Content to leave him full and safe, Lumina walked to where Ember danced, the goblin following just behind her. The salamander's dance slowed as she drew near the fire. By the time she had reached the circle of white stones, he was facing her, his dance having stilled to a sinuous sway. His eyes still looked through her as if she were not there. All the same, he spoke to Lumina as soon as she stood in front of him.

"You have returned," he said.

"I have," she answered. "And if you will abide just a few moments longer, I will dance with you."

"If you will dance with me, Lumina, then I will certainly abide," the salamander said, his gaze focusing on her for a moment, before moving past her to the creature that stood just beyond. He said nothing. Taking up his dance once again, he leapt higher and higher until the fire's circle of light spread all the way to the edge of the rose's branches.

Lumina and the goblin returned to where Hoax waited. They came to the very edge of the branches, where the firelight met the soft darkness. There Lumina stopped, but the goblin continued on into the night.

"Crow," she called out. He looked back over his shoulder at her.

"Crow?" he said, rolling the word around as if tasting it. "Yes, that name will do."

Lumina flushed slightly, for it had been presumptuous of her to give him a name of her choosing, but she continued on.

"Do you believe me now?"

"Given the evidence, how can I not?" he agreed. "Do you intend to continue feeding him?"

"Continue feeding him?" she asked, slightly puzzled. The shell had still been more than half full of milk.

"Yes, the amount of milk that you have will only last a day, perhaps less," he explained.

"Oh," she said, dismayed. She had no experience with such things, and had not really thought of what the kitten's needs might be in the future. Her thoughts must have been plain on her face.

"So do you still plan on trying to raise him?"

"Of course," she said, there being no other answer that she was willing to give.

"And how will you feed him?" he wondered.

She did not say, but her resolve must have been evident because a small chuckle escaped from the goblin's beaked mouth.

"I see. Well there is nothing I can do about the debt you have brought on yourself this night, but it will only be for this night. From this moment forward, I will help you and you will accrue no additional debt. Consider it a gift," he said, and there seemed to be a weight to his words.

He turned back towards Hoax who shimmered and shifted in the moonlight. Where once a tousle-maned pony had stood, now was a large raven, stretching and shaking his wings, settling his feathers in place. Crow leapt lightly to the phooka's back, the long tails of his black great coat blending with the midnight colored plumage so perfectly that they almost seemed of a piece. He looked down at her and she thought that he might have smiled, though it was difficult to tell with a visage such as his.

"Do not worry overly much about your debt to the Goblin King," Crow said. "He often has his mind turned to more pressing matters, and mayhap he will never collect. I will see you at moonrise tomorrow." And with that, Hoax launched them into the sky.

Lumina did not stay to watch in which direction they flew. Instead she turned, walking back to where Ember was waiting for her in the circle of white stones.

The wood she had left for him had long ago turned to ash, but that mattered not at all to a salamander if he wished to stay. Still, it was courteous to provide him with more, as a hostess would provide her guests with food and drink. So she added more wood to the circle, Ember taking care not to come too close as she did.

"Sweet one," he said, picking up a small twig and watching as it turned to ash in his fingers. "I am sure you know your own business, but I would offer you some advice; beware of goblin gifts. Much like fairy gifts, they rarely come free."

"Oh, I am sure there will be a price," she said, tossing him a small twig which he caught. It too quickly turned to ash, leaving behind a wonderful piney scent. "Still, I worry less about the gifts I have yet to be given than the debts I have already gained."

Had Lumina stayed to watch in which direction the raven and his passenger had flown, she might have seen them circle back to land just above her on one of the lone pine's sheltering branches.

Slipping off Hoax's back, the goblin squatted down on the branch next to where the phooka was perched. Neither the distance nor the foliage were obstacles that could stop him from seeing where the fairy and salamander were dancing below. The two moved in perfect harmony around the circle of stones, the elemental within and the sprite without, flames flashing in the air between them as she tossed small offerings to the salamander. The wind carried the sweetly scented smoke up to the branch where he and the phooka sat.

Hoax leaned forward so that his eye was on a level with the goblin squatting next to him. He cocked his head so that one eye looked down on the dancers below while the other looked on the face of his companion.

"An interesting sprite," commented the phooka.

"Yes," his companion replied.

"And was the milk that her kitten lapped up so readily

slated for the Goblin King's table?" he asked, still eyeing his companion.

"It was."

"Ah," said the phooka, turning his full attention back to the sprite below. "That will bring trouble."

"I am sure it will."

"It has been half a century since one of the fairy trespassed against us so blatantly. One wonders if it was softness or speculation that stayed your hand."

The phooka's comment was met only with silence.

"And apparently I will continue to wonder," he sighed. "Still, she seemed quite anxious about the kitten, and then there is the elemental. Do you think he is here by his will or someone else's? Could she have bound him?"

Again he was met with silence. The phooka sighed again, and ruffled his feathers.

They stayed and watched as the night grew older, until the dance reached its natural end. The dancers stood facing each other. The sprite reached up and plucked a single hair from her head, a shimmering strand of midnight blue which she tossed to the salamander.

He caught it and for the briefest instant it lay in his palm, then with a flash of emerald light it was gone. But, in its place was left a scent, a lovely scent like the air just before a summer storm, sharp and clean and filled with life.

"Ah, so that answers that question," said Hoax. "Still, I doubt it is much of a hardship being bound to her. What do you think, Crow," he asked, drawing out the name

Lumina had given to the goblin next to him. "Should I try it and see?"

"And what would a fairy maid do with one such as you?"

"Why, every goblin knows that answer; she would do what all maids are want to do! Pluck out my eyes and break my heart in two!" he finished with a flourish of wings and what might have been a grin on his raven's face.

The sylphs came the next morning, to run their fingers through the kitten's fur and tickle his whiskers. A storm followed close on their heels, bringing with it pouring rain and shrieking winds. It was fierce enough that even the rose's sheltering branches could not keep them dry.

Such things had never concerned Lumina before; she took joy in clear skies and thunderstorms alike, and had never had to worry about it one way or the other. But seeing the kitten huddled piteously in his nest, getting wet yet again, she could not revel in the storm's might as she usually would.

They couldn't stay where they were. Urging the kitten to his feet, she had him follow her deeper under the wild rose. There the thick, gnarled base twisted and twined about itself, forming a woody bower, its floor carpeted with old petals and leaves.

It was much drier there, though the winds still found them. That turned out for the best, however, because when next the sylphs visited, Lumina asked Zephyr, whose breath was much warmer than the others', if she would dry the kitten's fur. Of course, she was only too happy to do so, running her fingers through the silvery strands until not a single drop of water remained.

Once the kitten was dry, he began to mew softly; he was hungry once again. Reassuring him that she would be right back, Lumina went to where they had slept the night before. The milk in the turtle shell was somewhat diluted by the rain, but she doubted the kitten would mind.

The going was slow, but she was able to push the shell back to where he waited. Apparently he did not mind that the milk was a little watery, or he was hungry enough not to care, because when she brought it to him, he drank it down half way and promptly fell asleep.

Lumina left him that way, slipping up to the very top of the wild rose.

The storm still howled, roiling gray clouds filled in the sky above. The wind whipped the topmost branches about making them shy and dip like a ship on a restive sea. Lumina sat atop them with ease, paying them no mind as they bucked beneath her.

Instead, her thoughts turned back to the night before and her unexpected benefactor. She wondered if he would come at moonrise as he had said he would. And she wondered why he had decided to help her in the first place and what price that help had come at. But the weight of such wonderings soon left her. She was not really a creature built for brooding thoughts. Her nature was to find wonder and joy in everything, to dance to the world's song in all its many moods. So she let go of the questions that plagued her and laughed as the wind tossed her high in the air. And if thoughts of the kitten still occupied her mind and wove themselves into the never-ending song around her, she found that she did not mind at all.

The storm had become less fierce as the day went on until only a few wisps of clouds drifted through the setting sun's dying light. The winds too had gentled, though the sylphs still raced amongst the rose's branches, taking great delight in shaking water drops down on the heads of both Lumina and the kitten.

True darkness had fallen well before the moon began to rise. The turtle shell was long empty. Leaving it behind, she and the kitten made their way back to the outer edge of the rose. Now she stood with the kitten sitting next to her as she watched the darkness deepen, and contemplated what she planned to do about the empty shell if Crow did not keep his word.

She needn't have worried, because as soon as the moon showed her silvery head over the horizon, the flap of wings and a shadow passing overhead heralded their arrival. Lumina did not actually see the goblin approach, but from one heartbeat to the next, there he was, standing before her as if he had formed from the darkness itself.

The kitten did not seem surprised and began to purr as soon as he saw the goblin man. And despite the chills racing over her skin, Lumina was astonished to find that she too was happy to see him.

"At moonrise, as I promised," he said, giving her a small bow.

"As you promised," Lumina agreed, a smile blooming on her face.

She led him back towards where the empty turtle shell waited. The sylphs swirled around them, tugging at Crow's tattered coat tails, before racing up through the branches, a shower of water drops falling in their wake.

"*Aaah*, inconsiderate," Hoax squawked from his perch above them, rustling his now wet feathers in irritation. He hopped down to the ground, grumbling as he followed behind Lumina and Crow.

When they reached the wooden bower and the empty shell, Crow turned to Hoax. It was then that Lumina saw a satchel strapped across the phooka's chest. Crow reached inside the satchel, pulling out a white jug no bigger than a thimble. Unstopping it, he held it over the shell and began to pour. Out spilled a stream of pale milk.

The kitten did not wait for an invitation; he stuck his head in and began to drink, not caring if milk splattered on his face. And so it did, hanging like tiny pearls from the tips of his whiskers.

Milk continued to pour out of the jug long after it should have been empty; in fact, it kept pouring until the shell was filled to the brim. However, the kitten did not last as long. Flopping down as soon as his tummy was full, he fell fast asleep, not caring in the least that milk still dewed his whiskers and chin.

Lumina smiled at the sight, asking the rose for a few of its petals, which it gladly gave. She wiped the milk from the kitten's face.

"When they are this young they have yet to learn how

to clean themselves," Hoax said from just behind her.

Looking over her shoulder, she saw the phooka rummaging through the satchel on his chest with his beak. Eventually, he lifted out a brush with soft bristles and a handle made of ebony. He offered it to Lumina, but she did not reach for it.

"It is a gift, freely given," Crow assured her, taking the brush from Hoax's beak. He lifted Lumina's hand and gently placed the brush there. Reaching back into the satchel, he brought out a comb of carved bone. With it, he began to groom the kitten's fuzzy coat. Lumina joined him.

The gibbous moon passed overhead as they quietly brushed the kitten's silver fur. The night wind sighed through the pine boughs above them all the while, singing a gentle lullaby.

The night was old now; the kitten lay curled up in his bed of rose petals and dried leaves, safe in the rose's woody bower. Lumina stood watching over him, Crow's dark form standing at her side.

"Your salamander does not come to dance with you every night?" he asked.

"No, not every night, and I did not think it polite to call him out in the wet," she answered.

"Perhaps it would be good if you did," said Crow. "Creatures as young as your kitten need the warmth."

"Perhaps I will," she agreed, nodding her head. "The sylphs tell me the night wind said there is no more rain to come until well past dawn, so mayhap he will not mind my request."

"I am sure the request would trouble him not at all," Crow bowed to her. "Goodnight, Lady of the Glade. Until tomorrow." Turning, he walked out into the dark.

"Good night, fair one," Hoax said, giving her an elegant, yet comical bow, his wings spread out to either side. "And know that there are few who would deny you, especially if dancing with you would be their reward. Please remember this if ever you have need of a service from me." With a wink, the phooka turned, following Crow out into the darkness.

Crow and Hoax sat in the branches above, just as they had the night before, watching the sprite gather the white stones and move them back to where the kitten now lay sleeping. They saw the bird's nest she had used as a sling, sacrificed to give the salamander something to dance on. They watched her take a pinch of ash from a box and sprinkle it over the waiting wood. In no time at all, the salamander was dancing among the twigs, enticing Lumina to join him.

"Ah, so she can summon him," Hoax said. "Sylphs do her favors and salamanders come when she calls. I had thought your naming her as Lady of the Glade a flattery, but perhaps you spoke a truth."

"You wonder, yet you offered her your service," Crow pointed out.

"So I did. I thought it a good idea as you cannot," said Hoax.

"And you think I wish to?"

"I am beginning to think that you may be beginning to think that you might want to," said the phooka mischievously.

Crow sighed. "You could make a straight road twisted. There is no guile in her and I believe she truly cares for the kitten."

"So are we going to continue bringing milk for the kitten?" Hoax asked.

"Yes, for the time being," answered Crow.

"You need not bring it yourself," said Hoax. "If you prefer, I can easily bring it on my own."

"No, I will continue to come with you," Crow said, never taking his eyes off the figures dancing below.

"As you wish," replied Hoax, bowing his head slightly.

The sky had just begun to silver with the coming dawn when Lumina finally curled up with the kitten, while the salamander lay stretched out amongst the coals. It could be that he saw the black raven winging off to the west, heading away from the rising sun, or just as easily not; elementals rarely see the world as others do.

CHAPTER 3

Summer Winds and Winter Snows

The sun's light stretched out over the glade in long golden rays, proclaiming that the end of summer was near. Beneath the trees the sylphs were amusing themselves by spinning up a small whirlwind. Catching up little beech leaves in its breath, and standing them all on end so that they twirled about like tiny dancers. Round and around they spun as they moved in a wide circle. From shadow, to light, to shadow again they whirled, flashing through the sun dapples on the forest floor.

And in the center of all of this was the silver kitten, staring at the leafy dancers with serious intent.

On a branch above them, Lumina lay with her chin in her hands, watching as the leaves skittered away every time the kitten tried to pounce, smiling as she watched the little creature. The sun made his fur, which was still quite fuzzy, into a nimbus of bright silver.

A now familiar shadow passed over her, closely followed by the rustle of wings and a weight settling on the branch where she sat. The raven towered over her. From its back leapt a figure as black as the bird itself, the tails of his coat flaring and flapping as he landed lightly next to her. She greeted the pair fondly, as Crow sat tailor-fashion on the branch beside her. Since that first night when they had helped bring milk back to the kitten, not a day had gone by when she had not seen them. Their dark figures had become as commonplace in the glade as Lumina's own. The goblin's fearsome visage was now a welcome sight to her eyes.

Completely happy now, a dreamy languor settled over her as she looked back down to where the sylphs and the kitten played. The leaves continued to spin round and round, mesmerizing in their dance.

"They remind me of the revel the Fairy Queen holds on Midsummer's Eve," she said, more to herself than to the silent figure next to her.

"Have you danced in the Fairy Queen's round?" he asked, and Lumina wondered at the stillness in his voice.

"Once, when last the court came along through this doorway to Underhill," she said.

"And how long ago was that?" he asked.

"How long ago? I don't know. I don't often pay much attention to time. But I was still young, and had just planted the wild rose, so no more than a century ago, I would say. Why?" she asked, her attention now fully his.

"Because he wonders if you would have been there when last he had played for the fairy court," Hoax answered for him.

"You played for the court?" she asked Crow, but once again it was Hoax that answered.

"Oh yes, before the Goblin King sat on his obsidian throne, when there was but one court in Faerie. He would play his fiddle, and both the ring within and the ring without would turn to his tune, his music spinning them round and round and round again," the phooka said, sounding quite pleased with himself for some reason.

"Truly?" Lumina asked in wonder, finding it hard to picture the tall black figure beside her amongst the shining court of the Fairy Queen.

"Truly," Crow answered for himself this time, and though his answer to her was gentle, the eye he turned towards Hoax was as sharp as a blade. The phooka rustled his feathers, settling himself into silence.

When Crow turned back to Lumina, she saw the white fires dancing once again in the depths of his black eyes. For a moment, it was as it had been the first night they had met, and she was caught as a moth to a flame, not knowing whether or not it was her own destruction that beckoned her, yet unable to turn away.

"I would gladly play for you," he said, in a voice as soft as a night breeze, "if you would dance for me."

A desire to do just that swept through her. Her fears disappeared suddenly, like ghosts with the coming of dawn.

"Certainly," she said.

He reached out, gathering some twigs and a bit of spider's silk from near where they sat. She watched as his long fingers cleverly twisted them all into the semblance of a fiddle. As he wrapped the last strain of silk, the goblin's creation became a fiddle in truth. This was not just a glamour, but a true metamorphosis, and she marveled at it. The power of making was a deep, compelling magic that changed the warp and weft of the world. She wondered for the first time why a being such as Crow would spend his time with her and her silver kitten.

Finished, Crow stood, balancing on the swaying branch as easily as if he stood on bedrock. With one eye on her, he set his bow to string and began to play.

From one note to the next, the song of the world shifted, following the fiddler's tune. Laughing, Lumina rose up from where she lay, the call of the music one she could not deny, even had she wanted to. Her feet flashed with every golden note as she danced her reel. The joy that filled her felt as warm as the late summer sun.

The magic gathered to his tune, as he knew it would. What he had not known was how the sprite dancing before him would take all that he gathered and with each step, each sway, weave it into a glittering web that touched all near it, giving it life. Her dance was time-less and eternal. Joy was in every movement she made, in every flourish of her gossamer skirts, and every flair of her moth-wing coat. The sun kissed her honeyed skin and the golden threads on her hem, setting them aglow in its light, as if the sun itself could not help but shine the brighter in her happiness.

The phooka leaned down, his raven head appearing beside him. "She could have us all playing to her tune, if she but knew the power she had," he said for Crow's ear alone. "I would certainly play an eternity for her, if she would but dance throughout that eternity for me."

Crow held his tongue and continued to play. The phooka's words rang true, though he feared to admit it, because in his heart of hearts, he knew he would do the same.

A snow storm greeted the dawn of the winter solstice. All through the night, Lumina had heard the winds blowing. Normally, she would have slept the cold season through, curled up amongst the bare brambles of winter or in the boughs of an evergreen. But not this winter, with a young cat, not yet a year old, trailing along in her footsteps.

So now they were tucked up in a warm, dry den, far beneath the roots of Old Father Pine. The floor was lined with rose petals and wild thyme. And in one corner was a nest of cattail fluff and feathers, brought in before the snows by Crow and Hoax. The turtle shell sat near a hearth made of stone where Ember danced. The smoke from the flames curled up a small tunnel that served as a chimney, twisting out through the old pine's roots. A door made of birch bark covered the entrance of a larger tunnel, keeping in the fire's warmth.

Lumina watched Ember dance as she lay contentedly, snuggled up next to the young cat who lay sprawled in his nest, oblivious to the world. He had grown so quickly since the summer, and was now three times as long as she was tall. In fact, she could almost fit under his chin when he stood. She smiled to herself. Their little den was peaceful and mostly quiet, save for when the sylphs would race down through the small chimney. They whistled and laughed as they swirled around Ember, causing him to flare brightly for a moment, before racing out the larger entrance, banging the birch bark door behind them as they left.

They did this often at first, until Lumina pointed out that if the young cat froze to death, he would no longer be able to chase leaves with them. After that, they only came in every once in a while, but they still raced past the door tapping on it and calling out to her as they blew passed.

It was still early morning when Lumina heard a tapping on the door that did not come from the wind. The tapping was quickly followed by a raven's feathered head.

"Bright and happy morning to you, fair one," said Hoax, his large body filling the doorway. Suddenly, he let out a squawk and hopped all the way inside, flakes of snow scattering everywhere as he ruffled his wings in indignation. Crow followed in behind him, a hand full of downy black feathers held tightly in one fist.

"Something more with which to line the kitten's nest," he said, handing them to Lumina with a slight bow.

"What did you do that for?" asked Hoax, feathers still fluffed in outrage.

"For standing in the doorway while others waited out in the snow," answered Crow.

"Can I be blamed if the Lady's beauty had rendered my feet motionless?" said Hoax giving a little bow in Lumina's direction.

"A shame it cannot render you speechless," said Crow as he pulled the now familiar earthenware jug out from the satchel hanging around Hoax's neck. He went over to the turtle shell, and pulling the stopper from the mouth of the jug, began to pour the contents into the shell. He continued to pour until it was full to the brim with milk.

"The milk will warm in a little while," he said, fitting the stopper in the jug once more. He came over to sit near Lumina, handing her a packet as he did. When she opened it, she found that it held a bit of the brown bread with honey she loved so much.

Still grumbling, Hoax came to join them.

They settled in, sitting close together as the sleepy fire wrapped them in its warmth. The falling snow shushed the world above, until even the moaning of the wind was quieted. Lumina shared the bread and honey that had been brought to her, watching the firelight shimmer across the surface of the milk as she ate. The deep shadows cast by the soft light invited one to share confidences, and ask questions not usually asked.

"Hoax," she said, in a voice as soft as the fire's glow. "Why is there such enmity between your king and the Fairy Queen?"

Much to her surprise, it was Crow who answered.

"Because long before the Goblin King was the Goblin King, he was a knight of the Fairy Queen's court," he said, turning his dark gaze on Lumina. "She was his beloved, and he, one of her favored. But then there came a time when she believed that he had betrayed her. In a rage, she blinded him and banished him to exile. For a hundred years he endured, the love that had burned brightly for his queen turning to bitter ash." His voice held no rancor or judgment as he told the story, but the white fires that burned in the depths of his black eyes were as cold as starlight.

"He was blind and alone for a hundred years?" she said, her heart weighing heavily in her chest.

"Not entirely alone. There was one who followed him faithfully, a loyal servant who helped him as best he could. And others joined him," Crow continued. "Until he had a court and a kingdom of his own. Now none of the Fairy Queen's subjects will lightly trespass in his domain save for a certain desperate sprite who decided that saving a kitten was worth the possibility of starting a war."

"A war?" she said incredulously, believing perhaps that she had misheard the goblin.

"Yes, Lady of the Glade, if it had been deemed that you were sent by your Queen to steal the goblin's tribute, or even if you had done so with her knowledge, then it would have been war," Crow assured her. "But she did not send you, and so it is only you who owes a debt to the Goblin King. Do you still feel that it was worth it, I wonder?"

"Oh yes," Lumina said, fondly stroking the kitten's fur once again. "He has become very dear to me, and now I could not imagine my world without him."

All was silent for a while. Lumina could not help but think of the blind knight, maimed and exiled from all he knew by the one whom he had loved the most. To be alone, cast out and left to your fate without a care. A deep sadness filled her and she felt an intense need to hug the young silver cat laying next to her. So she did, resting her cheek against his soft fur, taking comfort in knowing that he was safe and alive.

"What betrayal could be so terrible, Crow?" she asked. "What could be so unforgivable, that she would do such a thing to one who had loved her so?"

He did not answer; he only sat watching her with his inscrutable eyes. The firelight danced across his coal-black feathers as the moment stretched on and on. Until she began to wonder if there would be any answer at all. Finally, he spoke.

"Sometimes, my sweet sprite, even a small betrayal can seem as vast as the sea," he said softly. "More so when love is concerned. And that begs the question, have you never been in love, Lumina?"

"I don't know," she answered truthfully. "I certainly have those that are dear to me. And there are those I miss when I do not see them, but it wasn't until the kitten came that any one being so consumed my thoughts."

"That is love, in the same fashion as how a mother feels for her child," he said. "But, a love such as the one the Goblin King once had for the Fairy Queen, that is a much different love. Such a love is like the sun, warm and golden. It fills your world and your heart basks in its light. But when that sun is taken away, the heart becomes a barren thing where nothing will grow save bitterness and thorns. And after a while not even those."

There was nothing she could say to that, so she said nothing at all. But she reached out to touch the hem of

Crow's coat, though she could not say why she felt the need to do so.

It was at that moment that the sylphs came racing down the chimney.

"Come see, come see," they cried, swirling about the room, stroking Ember awake so that the fire rose higher and higher.

"The snow has stopped!"

"The sun has returned!"

"Everything is white and it sparkles! Come out with us, come out and see!"

The sylphs made to leave by the birch bark door as they had done so many times before. But it refused to budge until Gale raced back out through the chimney to blow away the snow that had covered it.

The sylphs' excitement swept away the sorrow. Lumina stood, reaching out her hand to Crow who took it with what she thought might have been surprise. Together they slipped out through the door and into the cold clear morning.

The world was covered in pure white, just as the sylphs had said. A perfect blanket of snow that sparkled like stardust in the sun. Its brilliance was only broken here and there by the pale blue shadows of the trees.

Delighted, Lumina danced out over the pristine landscape. Out of the glade and across the meadow she went, all the way down to the water's edge, leaving not a single footprint behind her.

The frozen lake was a black mirror, an unblemished reflection of the clear blue winter sky. While Serene was deep beneath the ice, playing in her garden, Mistral and Gale raced across the surface, conjuring up little flurries of snow to swirl in their wake.

A shadow was standing beside her when she came to the lake's edge, and she found that she was holding onto Crow's hand still, having never let it go. It was almost as pale as the snow and tipped with talons like long obsidian blades, but his grip was warm and gentle. Smiling up at him, she took his other hand in hers and led him out onto the ice. They glided across the surface as easily as the sylphs. The two figures swooped and soared across the sky's reflection in the mirror of the lake's face, like birds in flight. They moved in perfect harmony until he broke away from her with a frightening suddenness, spinning and ducking as a smattering of white scattered across the ice in the place where he had just been.

On the near shore, Hoax stood laughing while snowballs rained down around Crow like arrows in a siege.

"Ha! That's what you get for pulling my feathers," said the phooka flapping his own wings for emphasis.

"I'll pluck you bald if you don't stop," warned Crow, deftly avoiding all that was thrown at him.

"Ah, but it isn't me," said Hoax, once again holding up his wings and thus showing why he could not be the one responsible. "Look to the sylphs," he said, gesturing off to his side.

"At your behest, goblin," said Gale.

"True enough; but still, it is not m…" Hoax spluttered, cut off mid-word as a snowball hit him unerringly in his open beak.

Perhaps that was why the phooka did not notice the little silver shadow, doing its best to be stealthy as it crept across the snow. The second snowball was most likely the reason he did not see that same shadow as it launched itself towards him.

In a heartbeat, the scene changed from a young cat trying to hold on to a raven's tail feathers to one doing his best not to let go of a stomping pony's mane.

"Ah, you little…" the phooka snorted, shaking his mane in an effort to dislodge the young cat. "I'll take you back down into the lake you came from if you do not let go!"

"You will do no such thing, phooka!" said Lumina, her voice strident. The tableau froze as all stopped and looked at her in surprise.

"But, Lady!" Hoax pleaded, the kitten still hanging on to his mane with teeth and all four claws.

"You will not hurt that kitten!"

"What about him hurting me?" the phooka pleaded, and when it seemed that there was no sympathy in the offing he sighed with resignation.

"Fine," he said. Then he was a raven again, his tail feathers still clamped in the kitten's teeth. He reached back and pecked the young cat between the ears. "Let go!" he admonished.

"But I caught you fair and square!" the young cat insisted around a mouthful of feathers.

"And what do you think you are going to do with me?" the phooka asked.

"I don't know," the young cat admitted. "Eat you, I guess."

CHAPTER 4

The First Day of May

"You know, Mistress, that it is raining," the silver cat said from where he was sitting beneath a tangle of rose stems. He was doing his best to stay dry even though little raindrops fell all around him, flashing like diamonds in the morning light.

"Did you know that it was on this day, the very first day of May, that I found you?" asked his mistress. She danced out beneath the open sky, the sun-shower surrounding her in a glittering curtain of falling rainbows. "In almost the exact same place you sit now."

"Yes," the silver cat answered, "but it is still raining." He waited and when it was obvious that no reply was forthcoming, added, "Which means it is wet."

"Yes, dearest, it is wet," his mistress agreed. "It often is when it rains."

He blinked incredulously at her.

"Do you want to get wet?" he asked, his ears pointing off to either side of his head, like a pair of horns. She just laughed fondly at him. A shadow passed overhead, soon followed by a large raven coming to rest on an old log, laying not far from where his mistress danced.

"Hoax," the silver cat called out, perking up at the arrival of a potential ally. "It's raining," he stated.

"So it is," answered the phooka, fluffing his feathers.

Clearly, the phooka was insane too.

"Hoax!" his mistress exclaimed. "It has been forever since we last saw you! Where have you been?"

"Seven nights, to be precise, my sweet sprite. But a better question would be, how could I stay away, knowing such a greeting awaited me on my return! No, no. Keep your kisses and warm embraces and claims of broken hearts ever-lasting!" the phooka teased. "Scoldings are how one truly shows their love!"

"Don't be foolish," his mistress admonished. "A day has not gone by in this last year that we did not see you. Can you blame me for being worried?" She spun past the phooka, reaching out to touch his talon as she did so. "Is Crow not with you?"

The silver cat looked around, and sure enough, the familiar figure in a tattered long coat was missing.

"He is not, sweet sprite! Although I am sure he would prefer to be. With you at least, if not me. But don't worry, he will join us when he can," promised Hoax.

The silver cat grumbled. "That is all well and good, but it is still raining."

Crow arrived just after the sun had passed midday. The rain had stopped, leaving only a few clouds sailing lazily across the summer blue sky. In the meadow, a honeysuckle vine hung swing-like between two tall grasses. It was there that Lumina and the goblin sat, swaying gently in the wind as they ate bread and honey.

Their shadows lay stretched out in front of them, growing longer in the lowering sun.

"So Hoax took the scolding meant for me?" Crow asked, as he passed her another piece of bread.

"I did not scold him! But it has been odd not having you both here every day," Lumina admitted. "Not hearing the silver cat and Hoax bicker. And I missed you not being here to play your fiddle as I danced."

"And I would rather have been here to play for you. Unfortunately, we are not always free to choose as we would wish to. There are whispers from the Fairy Queen's court, rumors that if true, may mean you will see even less of us in the days to come," he said. "But today is not tomorrow, and if you are willing, there is a place I would like to take you. But fair warning, it is in the goblin's wood."

"Wasn't it just this winter that you warned me of what the consequences would have been, had I been caught taking the tribute meant for the goblins?"

"So it was, and as I remember it, the goblins did catch you," Crow pointed out.

"So they did," she said, her face warming when she realized that she no longer thought of Crow as such. "Then I would think I should be even more cautious. I am sure they would find me being in their wood to be an even greater trespass. And if we're caught..."

"But you won't be caught," he promised, and Lumina believed him. She found his mood a strange one though; somber, yet playful at the same time. As though he knew a secret that much amused him, but that he would not share. "So will you come with me?"

Despite whatever secrets he may or may not have, she trusted him, and acquiescing, nodded her agreement.

"Shall we go then?" he asked. "And no need to worry, the silver cat knows his way very well."

"Does he now?" she said, her thoughts about secrets disappearing as the laughter bubbled up inside her. "And how would you know that?" she asked the silver cat who lay sleeping in a sunbeam not far from where they sat.

"Well, where else was I to hunt?" he pointed out, yawning hugely. "You promised all of the creatures here that I wouldn't eat them."

A short time later, they left the glade. Hoax glided overhead, Crow seated between his wings. Below them, the silver cat bounded along, Lumina astride his sleek back. She held on tightly to his fur as he leapt lightly from stone to stone, across the rushing stream which served as the border between the fairies' wood and that which belonged to the Goblin King. The sun glittered on the frothing water and wet stones, disappearing behind them as they entered the dark wood on the other side.

Wych-elm and oak grew everywhere; thick-boled giants, their fingers interlaced so tightly that twilight had already fallen beneath their branches. Their knobby feet rose up from the leaf strewn forest floor in great twisting pathways.

The shadows here were deep and alive, compelling, and strangely beautiful. Where in her glade the wind sang, here it whispered, telling of old secrets, forgotten promises, and centuries long gone.

They went deep into the wood where a small clearing

opened up in front of them. There, the long rays of the late afternoon sun speared through the trees, setting the carpet of forget-me-nots stretching out before them aglow with its honeyed light. The shadows by contrast were sharp-edged and deep. At its center stood an ancient pile of stones bathed in a nimbus of gold.

The silver cat carried her to the foot of it. Lumina realized they were at the base of an old, old well. A tangle of roses grew along its crumbling walls. The ancient canes were covered in blossoms of the palest pink, now gilt-edged with the setting sun.

She did not hear Hoax land, but when she looked down, Crow was standing at her knee, a hand stretched out to her. She took it, sliding down from the silver cat's back to stand beside him. She followed him up the mossy stones, reaching out to stroke the gilded leaves as she passed. Just as with the wood, the roses too whispered of secrets, but these were of soft touches and stolen kisses and gentle, loving laughter.

When they reached the top, she left Crow trailing behind as she walked to the rim of the well. She peered over the edge, and marveled at what she found. Instead of reflecting the vibrant pinks and fiery golds of the sky above them, the water, if water it was, shone the deepest black. In its depths, countless fires burned, cold and white, forever falling into an endless void.

"What is this place?" Lumina asked her silent companion.

"The Well of Stars," he answered from just behind her. He too reached up to stroke one of the rose's soft petals. "Once, long ago now, this was the trysting place for two lovers. The woman was strong-minded, beautiful... and mortal. Her lover was a knight in the Fairy Queen's court."

"The roses still speak of their laughter," she said, turning around, only to find he had moved away.

He said no more. The silence stretched out between them, filled only by the wind's eerie song and the rose's soft whispers. She wondered once again at the strangeness of his mood and what had moved him to bring her to this place.

Dusk fell and deepened towards true night as he drifted along, reaching out occasionally to stroke a thorny stem. She followed in his wake, content as always to listen to the singing of the world around them.

The stars were bright overhead when his thoughts seemed to return from wherever they had been. He did not turn to look at her when finally he did speak, only continued in ceaseless wandering.

"You told me once that you danced in the Fairy Queen's round."

"I have," she answered, not sure where this odd humor would take them.

"Would you dance with me now?" he asked, still not turning towards her.

She stopped, not sure if she had heard him correctly.

In a blink, he was before her, a towering dark figure. The wind tugged at the tails of his coat as its shadows reached out to embrace her. The pale fire of his eyes burned brightly, as they had that very first night. But she held no fear of them now.

"Come dance with me, Lady of the Glade," he said. Simple words, but spoken in a voice that stoked the fires in her cheeks and made ice run cold through her veins.

She reached out and took his hand in hers. Together they glided over the crumbling stones, dancing round and around as the stars wheeled in the sky above them. The forget-me-nots sighed and the bluebells rang as the night wind played through them, a soft symphony. The trees creaked in eerie counterpoint; a melody both haunting and lovely as it rose and fell, mesmerizing.

Together, apart, and together again, their bodies ensnared in the timeless waltz. Closer and closer they came together with each return, until there was nothing to stand between them. She felt the softness of his coat, and the world's song running beneath her skin. They moved as one, breathed as one, their hearts in perfect harmony.

"Crow," the word pierced through the music of the wood like a spear, shattering the eternal moment through which they moved. Their dance had ceased, but Crow still held her close.

"*Crow!*" Hoax said again, his words sharp. "A troop is coming, Pax's, I think."

Lumina's partner sighed and stepped away from her.

"It would be best if they did not see you here," he said, as the silver cat leapt up to the wall beside them.

"You should not have brought me if it would bring trouble to you," said Lumina.

"It has brought no trouble, nor will it. But even if it had, I would have thought the trouble worth it," he said, taking her hand in his and turning it over. He pressed something into her palm, gently closing her fingers over it.

"It would be best if you were to go now," he said, his thumb brushing across her wrist. "Hoax, go with her. I will stay and contend with Pax."

"Be well, Lady of the Glade," Crow said softly. He turned and faded into the gloom, his coat tails fluttering behind him like wings.

She did not take the time to look at what was in her palm. Vaulting to the silver cat's back, she held on as he sprang away, back the way they had come. Hoax, a shadow among shadows, flew silently above them.

They saw no one on their return journey. Soon they were padding quietly though the glade once more. All around them, moonlight gathered in silver pools on the forest floor. The night wind played a familiar lullaby through the branches of Old Father Pine. They were home. Finally, she opened her hand to see what it was that Crow had put there.

Nestled in her palm was a ring like nothing she had ever seen before. So cleverly worked, it looked as if someone had plucked the moon down from the sky, wrapped it in a bramble of silver roses, and made it small enough to fit on her finger. If she looked closely, she could even see tiny ravens flying amongst the thorny vines. Blue phantasms chased violet across the face of the tiny moon, as silvery white shadows shifted in its depths. It was breathtakingly intricate.

She slipped it onto the middle finger of her heart hand. It fit as if it had always been there. She rubbed her fingers over the smooth, cool stone, finding comfort in it.

"A moon to light our moonless night. Promises. Promises. I guess we'll soon see," a voice said from beside her.

She looked up to find Hoax there, looking down at her with glittering black eyes.

"I've seen you safely home and now I return to save Pax from the price of a dance interrupted. Take care, sweet sprite. May the days fly by till we see you again."

With that he was off, flying out into the night before she had a chance to ask him just what it was he had meant, in all his foolishness.

CHAPTER 5

The Fairy Queen's Round

Lumina had never really noticed the passage of time. Of course, she noticed the seasons change and that night turned into day, that things were born, grew and died, but never before had it dragged like a stone tied to her heel. She was ever conscious of it now, and had been since the first day of May.

Despite Hoax's best wishes, the days did not fly by, and the goblins' absence was a plague on her thoughts. She drifted through each day with a strange melancholia twining itself tighter and tighter around her heart.

Ember came to dance with her almost every night, and the sylphs often kept her company, though playing with the silver cat was more likely their true motivation. They never seemed to tire of running their fingers through his fur or spinning leaves over the ground and up in the air for him to chase. When he deigned to do so, of course.

Sometimes, she would sit with the Rowan Maiden, listening as she shared gossip that her birds had brought to her. Swift often joined them, sharing news of the wider wood as he watched his family graze in the meadow beyond.

Or, Lumina would head down to the lake's edge to visit the nixy, the silver cat reluctantly in tow. There she would sail rose petal boats over the green water while

Serene would push fish up onto the shore in the hopes that the silver cat would let her pet his fur.

But mostly Lumina would find herself stretched out on the stems of the wild rose, the heavy clusters of blossoms nodding around her, the green leaves, toothy and edged in red, shading her like a canopy. There she would lay, watching the sky beyond them with its ever moving clouds, thinking about the ring on her finger with its auroras and shadows, and wondering what had happened to the one who had given it to her.

And so she spent her days, until midsummer came.

The morning of Midsummer's Eve dawned clear and bright, setting everything aglow with a golden light. Thistledown floated on the winds blowing across the meadow, and amongst the swaying flowers, the fairies gathered.

The nixy left her lake and the Rowan Maiden her tree. Lumina sat atop her silver cat and Ember danced with the sylphs on the back of the wind. They laughed and sang as they searched for all manner of curious things, like feathers and fish scales and old dragonfly wings. They wrapped them up in spider's silk, twining them with rue and roses and sweet smelling clover to make masks for the night's revelry.

Dusk settled about them as they capered and played until purple twilight reigned. When the time came, they set off; through the meadow they danced, and through the glade with its graceful beech trees and sea of bluebells. Until finally, they came to an old hazel grove.

There, in its center, sat a great boulder split through its very heart. And from that crack spilled a beckoning light.

Merrily the revelers answered its summons. First went the sylphs and the salamander, next the nixy, then the dryad and finally came Lumina with her silver cat. They stepped through joyously, for almost a hundred years had passed since last this doorway had opened to Underhill and the Fairy Queen's court.

They left the mortal world behind, and everything changed. Lumina's dress was now of velvet evergreen. Her mask, no longer fish scales and rose petals twined in spider's silk, but crystals and garnets wrapped in spun gold. Her midnight blue hair caught up with long twisting strands of amber beads. But to her, perhaps the strangest thing of all was the silver cat, who now rode atop her shoulder, instead of her riding atop his.

They walked through a land where there were no shadows. Where slender boles of crystalline trees rose up like pillars from a floor of malachite. Their spreading branches held aloft a sky made of lapis. The trees opened up to a great circle where the Fairy Queen's round danced. Two rings of dancers there were, one within the other. The inner ring spun widdershins as sunwise spun the outer. And in its center, rising above all, was a dais. Upon it was a throne, where sat the Fairy Queen.

She was dressed in mist and sunlight with hair like a golden waterfall, and eyes the deep blue of a winter sky. At her feet sat a boy who was as beautifully golden as she, save that he was mortal. A very strange thing indeed.

Lumina did not join the dancers, not quite yet, stopping

instead at the edge of the trees. The outer ring, being the lesser ring, spun past just beyond the place where she stood. There was where the wild folk danced; elementals, pixies and sprites such as herself. Colorful and bright as butterflies on a breeze, they whirled past her in gleeful abandon, calling out for her to join them. Her feet willed her to do so.

Lumina reached up to stroke the silver cat's ears. "Dearest, I think it is best that you do not come with me into the round," she said to her companion. "Mortal things do not fare well in our dance."

The silver cat flicked his tail. "I doubt that I would come to any harm, but if it will make you happy I will find someplace else to be," he said, rubbing his head against her cheek. He leapt lightly to the ground, flicking her skirts with his tail as he headed off into the crystal wood.

She finally gave in to the pull of the dance, flowing into the outer ring without a ripple.

So turned the rings of the Fairy Queen's round, greater to lesser, widdershins to deasil, order to chaos, in perfect harmony.

And so they danced until the tolling of a great bell marked the midnight hour, bringing with it a feeling of portent. The world seemed to slow, as the air grew heavy and expectant, like the moment just before a great storm. Lumina wondered what it might herald as she saw the growing shadows gather in a place where there had but a moment ago been no shadows, beneath the crystal trees. From their dark depths came a host of goblins, great and small.

Astonishment shivered through the Fairy Queen's court at the sight, though the dancers never faltered. The faerie rings, both the greater and the lesser, continued to turn unbroken, as did the seasons themselves.

Lumina's eyes searched through the goblin host of their own accord, passing over its bogels, boomen and powries, henkies, glastigs and bodachs without stopping. She saw the blue face of muilearteach and brown fur of the wulver, but the familiar dark coat and feathered visage which she had hoped for, was nowhere to be seen. There was, however, another in the throng who caught and held her gaze. The Goblin King watched her as she spun past in a dance that now seemed infinitely slow. His eyes captured her as neatly as a butterfly in a net.

If the Queen's hair was sun gold, then his was starlight, falling heavy and straight over a coat of cobalt blue. Two silver antlers swept up and back from his brow. The planes of his face were sharp, his eyebrows straight and fine. His lips, beautiful and cold, held a small secret smile as he looked at her.

And then the dance swept past him, out of the reach of his smile though it lingered in her mind long after he was beyond her sight.

A painful fluttering filled her chest, like a million moths dashing themselves to pieces around her heart. After centuries of absence, could it be anything else but her trespasses that would bring the Goblin King back to the Queen's court?

And what of those goblins that had aided her? She had seen neither Crow nor Hoax amongst the host. Had in fact, not seen them since the first day of May. The night when she had danced with Crow along the edge of the Well Of Stars, deep in the goblin's wood.

Another of her trespasses, she recalled, as a thread of worry now wove itself into her growing fear. She could not help but wonder if their absence and their king's arrival had ought to do with each other.

Her eyes turned toward the dais where the Goblin King now sat near the Fairy Queen, on a throne carved from the night sky. And there, curled contentedly in his lap was the silver cat. The king's long, graceful fingers scratched gently behind the cat's ears.

This sight did not calm Lumina's roiling insides, however. Instead, it twisted them up further and filled her mind with a whirlwind of questions and fears. Thankfully, her feet did not need her head, so they continued to carry her on from partner to partner, deftly weaving her through the dance.

The Goblin King's throne had been placed close to the Fairy Queen's, though not too close. They were alone on the dais, save for the golden boy at her feet and the silver cat in his lap. He sat, stroking the soft fur idly as he waited. There was a game afoot, but it was the Queen's game and it was for her to make the opening move.

"I am pleased that you have joined our revel," said the Fairy Queen. Her voice was at once as light as birdsong, and as husky as a lover's whisper. "With so many past invitations having gone unanswered, I was not sure if you would attend."

"I was curious to see if it was as I remember it," he said, turning his eyes away from the revelers. "And it is... but for one small addition." He nodded his head at the boy sitting at the Queen's feet. "He is a lovely child."

"Yes," the queen agreed, reaching out to touch the boy's hair. "He looks so much like someone we knew, wouldn't you agree?" she asked, and although her head was inclined towards the boy, her wintry gaze was turned on the Goblin King.

"Mayhap," he replied neutrally, turning his attention back to the dancers.

The queen watched him with a small smile. They both knew it was his turn in their game, and there was no doubt what his move would be. Still, he sat in silence until she turned away, seeming to dismiss him, though he knew she had not.

He watched the kaleidoscope of dancers flash past him. The fae in their masks and the goblins without, the innermost ring spinning widdershins at the edge of where he sat. The masks they wore were strikingly beautiful, full of purity and innocence. He doubted the faces beneath them were the same.

His gaze drifted out further still to the ring turning sunwise just beyond, where the lesser fae danced. His goblins slid in to caper alongside them, like falling leaves amongst butterflies. The Greater of the fairy court paid them no mind, but he did. A small smile softened his lips as he watched them.

There was no sense to rush his move. So, he remained patient, letting hours pass before returning to the subject of the boy at the Fairy Queen's feet.

"I wonder what it would be like to have a mortal child in my court," he mused. "Would you consider giving him to me?" The Fairy Queen's lips curved like a hunter's bow.

"Give him to you?" she asked, her eyes lightening until they were the pale blue of a glacier's heart.

"Yes," he answered back. "A gifting to honor this time when our two courts danced as one."

"I would be loathe to lose him!" she exclaimed, stroking the boy's golden hair. "He reminds me of a time long ago when two lovely mortal men sat at my side, my Sun and my Moon, who brought such life to my court." She stared fondly down at the boy, who stared up at her with adoration.

"No, I don't think I could part with him, but perhaps..." she continued, locking her shrewd gaze with his, "it could be both ways. If you were to choose a bride from my court, then it could be as if he were not gone at all." A smile unfurled like a spring meadow across the Fairy Queen's face, her eyes now gleaming in triumph.

At last the game was becoming clearer to him. He leaned closer to her, his own smile full of implied promises as he asked.

"Any in your court?"

She leaned in as well, closing the distance between them till only a whisper separated them.

"Any in my court who will have you," she answered.

He stood as she sat back in her crystal throne, the silver cat jumping down lightly from his lap as he did so. Bowing his head to the Fairy Queen, the Goblin King stepped off the dais, and was swept up into the swirling round.

When next Lumina looked, the Goblin King was no longer on his throne and the silver cat was nowhere to be seen. Her heart seized in a panic until she heard a soft chime from above. Looking up she saw the silver cat stretched out on one of the pillar tree's crystal branches, lazily batting at the shining leaves.

Relief replaced panic as she let go of her partner's hand with her left, holding her right hand up high over her shoulder for her new partner to take. And so he did, deftly spinning her into his embrace.

Suddenly she found the dance had changed. No longer did she spin sunwise, but widdershins, the one who had taken her hand having drawn her over from the lesser ring to the greater as smoothly as water over sand. She was startled, yes, but somehow not surprised when looking up, she found it was the Goblin King who was looking back down at her.

Specters of color drifted across eyes as pale as the moon, silver shadows shifting in their depths.

"Lumina," he said, with a voice as soft as a night wind. "I believe you owe me a debt."

His eyes held her spellbound as her heart became a lead weight in her chest. Her fears resolved themselves to be true. The Goblin King was here as a result of her trespasses.

She saw again the image of the silver cat curled up in the Goblin King's lap. He had been worth it, whatever the cost. So if there was a price, she would pay it gladly, her and her alone.

"You are owed a debt," she acknowledged, meeting his gaze with her own steadfast one. "And I will pay it. Me and me alone. You cannot take him."

"I cannot take him?" he said, parroting her words back. His eyes grew stormy beneath his furrowed brow, then just as quickly they cleared. His smile softened, becoming, at least to her eyes, more sincere.

"I would never try to take the silver cat from you, Lumina, even if he would let me," he promised. "Nor would I ask you to bring harm to any living thing. But if I call upon you to grant me a boon this night, before the cock crows, will you? If it turns out that I ask nothing of you, then still I will consider you free of any debt you owe me."

She nodded her head, the relief she felt washing away any other questions that she might have thought to ask.

"Until then," he said, smoothly handing her off to another partner. She found herself once again in the lesser ring of the Queen's round, moving deasil in the familiar dance and wondering what more the night would bring.

The night grew older and the Queen's round continued to turn in its never-ending dance. Many a partner took up Lumina's hand, both goblin and fairy alike, but the Goblin King did not come to her again. Whenever her nerves would allow her to look, she would find him sitting on his throne, the silver cat now perched on his shoulder.

The evening was almost at its end, and he had yet to ask anything of her. She had begun to hope against hope that she might see this night through without him doing so, and yet still be free of her debt. It was almost dawn, when the cock would crow his welcome to the rising sun. It would not be long now.

A goblin man took up her hand and smiled at her with the most mischievously wicked smile. It shined impossibly wide and white in his youthful, handsome face. His skin was as pale as cream, and his hair was the color of coal. Two pointed ears, as furry and black as his hair, peaked up through the tousled mass.

"Lovely, lovely Lumina," he said, eyes of the palest green gleaming out at her from behind long, untidy bangs. "Stay close to me. Soon his majesty will ask his boon of you."

Fear rose from the pit of her stomach. The pointed ears atop the goblin's head flipped back, then forward again, and his smile, though still wicked, became more comforting.

"Do not fear, fair one, it will not be as bad as all that," he reassured her, drawing their linked hands to his heart in an unspoken promise.

It was at that moment that the queen stood and the rings stilled at her silent command. The faces of the revelers turning towards her like flowers to the sun.

"The Goblin King has expressed an interest in my page," she said, "and wishes him to enter his service. But, I am also very fond of him, and am loath to give him up. So, we have come to an agreement. If one from this court will consent to be his bride I will release the boy into their service. Remove your masks, so that he may choose from among you."

When the masks fell away so did their glamours, revealing the most unlovely, cruel, or uncouth of the Fairy Queen's subjects. Others, such as Serene and the Rowan Maiden, simply disappeared, returning to whence they had come. The masks they had worn having been tokens of the Fairy Queen's power, and thus the only means by which they could be so far away from their homes.

The Goblin King stood, the silver cat still perched on his shoulder. Nodding to the Fairy Queen, he turned to the crowd before him and gestured.

At his gesture, Lumina's partner strode boldly forward with her on his arm. He brought them to stand before the Goblin King. Bowing to his liege, he then knelt, leaving Lumina standing alone.

The Goblin King reached out, and taking both her hands in his, drew her up the steps of the dais until she stood on the top with him.

"Lovely sprite, I would beg a boon of you."

A band tightened around her heart as she stared up into his moonstone eyes.

"Will you consent to be my bride?" She stood, still as stone, knowing that there was only one answer she could give, yet unable to give it.

It was the gentle purring of the silver cat, still riding on the king's shoulder that broke the spell. She fell into a deep curtsy, and bowed her head in consent. But when she closed her eyes, it was Crow's dark visage she saw looking back at her.

Although the sprite whose hands he held could not see the face of the Fairy Queen, the Goblin King could. And for just a heartbeat, it had shone with her fury.

The queen was incensed. She had thought him neatly caught, believing that he would either be forced to take a wife of her choosing from amongst the cruelest and most unlovely of her subjects, or to choose to stand at her side once more.

Or it was possible that none would have had him, if it was his rejection and humiliation that the queen had sought above all else. That he might ask one of the lesser of her court to wed him had not even occurred to her.

When next he looked at the Fairy Queen, her face was the picture of happiness, as if this had been the best of all outcomes.

"Then as promised," she said, her voice warm and bright, "once you are married, I will give the boy over in service to your bride. Until then, I will keep him with me, but will bring him to her at least once every fortnight for training in his duties."

"Agreed," he said, then looked down at Lumina and asked, "What date would you set for the wedding?"

She stared up at him, her bright amber eyes wide. The cat perched on his shoulder purred even louder. She hesitated for a moment longer before answering.

"Hollentide Eve," she said, "when the fairies move their court."

He could not stop the smile that bloomed across his face.

"As you wish," he said, just as the cock's crow echoed through the hall, heralding the birth of the new sun.

It was dawn and the night's revel was at an end. The Goblin King offered her his arm, and Lumina accepted it. He led her down from the dais, and the crowd parted before him. The goblin man who had led her to meet her doom fell in behind them as did many, many others whom she thought might be knights and nobles of his court.

The rest of the goblin host passed by them, capering merrily through the crystal trees as they returned back to the shadows from whence they had come. Until finally she was left standing before the doorway through which she had entered Underhill, with only their king and his loyal knights at her side. Together, she and the Goblin King crossed over the threshold, stepping out into the hazel grove.

The wind danced through the beech leaves and set the bluebells a-ringing. It whispered through the soft needles of Old Father Pine. Everywhere the rustling of the glade hummed a joyful song, welcoming Lumina home.

She was once again her tiny self, the silver cat at her side, towering over her. The Goblin King and his knights were now giants by comparison. It would be no trouble at all for one of them to fit her in the palm of his hand. But between one breath and the next, they rippled and shrank, till they were more of a size to match her own. The Goblin King offered her his arm once again, and she accepted it, not knowing what else to do. Together they left the hazel grove, a curious procession led by a proud-tailed silver cat.

They followed him through the sea of bluebells that grew under the beech trees. His tail like a silver banner, leading them beneath the delicate blooming arches and beyond, to the mossy stones and the cleft boulder where the rowan grew. The Rowan Maiden watched them curiously, but said nothing as they passed. They continued on through the glade until they came to the wild rose. There the silver cat stopped, having decided it was as far as he wanted to go. Lumina stopped as well. The Goblin King stayed at her side, his knights continuing on a bit further before coming to a halt. He turned to her then, taking her hands up in his once again.

"I truly regret that you have become a part of this game the Fairy Queen plays with me. And yet, I cannot help but feel as though fortune has smiled on me," he said, bending his head and bringing her hand up to lightly brush the backs of her fingers with his lips.

He offered her a soft smile then and to her surprise,

it was filled with warmth and life, like a newly opened flower offering up its beauty to the sun.

"And though it was your debt to me that compelled you to accept my suit, I hope to woo and win you in truth. So that when you stand beside me on Hollentide Eve, it will be because your heart wishes it." His words sent her reeling like too much honeyed-wine.

He stepped back from her, towards the place where his knights awaited him, shadow and starshine shimmering in the air around him. When next she blinked, she found the Goblin King gone. In his stead stood a great white stag, his coat luminescent as a moonflower in the rising sun.

The stag nodded his noble head to Lumina and leapt away, the brilliant morning light rippling along his strong flanks as he disappeared into the shadows of the Goblin Wood.

CHAPTER 6

A Bride for the Goblin King

Lumina sat perched on a buttercup in almost the exact spot where the Goblin King had left her the day before.

She had not woven garlands of flowers on Midsummer's Day as she would have normally done, nor had she taken much notice when the silver cat had headed out on some errand of his own.

Instead she had sat and watched the wind run its fingers through the tall grasses, all the while wishing Crow would appear with his fiddle. That he would play and she would dance and that all would be as it had been.

But things were not as they had been, and he had not come. Neither had the silver cat who had yet to return. Lumina had never felt loneliness before. But that night, it wrapped around her like a fog as she sat listening to the wind sigh mournfully through the glade.

The sun's light was just turning from dawn's pale silver to the gold of morning when she saw two children walking hand in hand beneath the beech trees. One was a boy, the very boy she had last seen sitting at the feet of the Fairy Queen. And the other, was the Fairy Queen herself.

She appeared as a beautiful little girl. Soft brown ringlets bounced merrily against full cheeks as she and the boy walked towards the place where Lumina now stood waiting for them. Lumina curtsied to them gracefully from atop her buttercup.

"Good morning, little sister," the Fairy Queen greeted her, in a voice as high and lilting as a bird's. Eyes, large and sweet as a doe's, looked out at Lumina from a cherubic heart-shaped face. "We thought to come and visit."

The queen let go of the boy's hand so that she could run hers lightly over the flower-tops. She left him next to Lumina as she wandered deeper into the meadow that stretched out beyond the glade, and all the way down to the nixy's lake.

Lumina did not watch the queen as she went about her meanderings. Her attention was drawn to the boy. He remained exactly where the Fairy Queen had left him. A beatific smile stretched his lips wide, as he stood watching the world around them with empty eyes.

"Such a beautiful place you live in!" the queen said, as she reached out to neatly pluck a buttercup from its stem. "No doubt it will be difficult for you to leave it."

So intent was Lumina on the boy, that it took a moment for her to realize what it was that the Fairy Queen had said.

"Leave it?" she said, puzzled. Looking up at the queen who had wandered back to where they stood. "Why would I leave?"

The queen's dark eyes filled with a sad sympathy as she looked at Lumina.

"You are to be the Goblin King's bride," she pointed out gently. "And it would stand to reason, would it not, that Lorne would wish to keep his wife with him in the goblin city."

The Fairy Queen's words were hard to keep hold of, scattering through Lumina's mind like birds taking flight. Only one thing seemed to stay long enough for her to catch hold of.

"My Queen, who is Lorne?" she asked.

A kindly smile lit the queen's little-girl face. "Lorne is the Goblin King, my sweet sprite," she said, reaching out to take Lumina's hand. It looked tiny resting on the tip of the queen's child-like finger. The colors shifted ephemerally across the ring Lumina wore as the queen turned her hand this way and that.

"How thoughtless of him to give you such a token, but not his name," said the queen.

But of course, her ring had not come from the Goblin King, and Lumina was about to say as much when her eyes happened to fall on the boy. In that moment he somehow reminded her of the silver cat when she had first found him as a kitten, alone and dying beneath the branches of the wild rose. So she said nothing, keeping the truth of the ring's origin to herself.

The queen let go her hand, walking back out amongst the flowers. But Lumina could not seem to stop looking at the boy and wondering what it was about this mortal child that made the Goblin King want him so.

"Why does the Goblin King want the boy?" Lumina asked.

"For his blood," answered the queen, her chubby little hands once again running themselves lightly over the tops of the flowers.

"His blood?" Lumina echoed in bewilderment.

"Oh yes," the queen assured her. "The boy's mortal blood calls to him." Her dark eyes turned back towards Lumina, studying her in a very unchild-like way. "Why did he choose you?" the queen asked. "Out of everyone in my court, why you? Had you met before?"

"No, my Queen," Lumina answered honestly. "I had never met the Goblin King before that night."

"Then why did you not refuse him when he asked you for this boon?"

The desire to tell everything to the queen rested heavily on Lumina's tongue, compelling her to trust all her burdens to the powerful being before her.

A peal of laughter rang out from the broken boy. He had not moved from where the queen had left him. He just stood there, staring into the sun as he smiled and laughed at nothing at all. A deep sadness settled in Lumina's heart.

"I did not feel that I had a choice," was Lumina's only reply. Which, in and of itself, was the complete truth.

"If only the thought that he might ask you had come to me sooner! I would have certainly done things differently," said the Fairy Queen, her countenance once again filled with concern. "You should have no part in this affair. Would that I could remove you from it," she said sadly, reaching out a fingertip to stroke Lumina's arm in a sisterly fashion. "The goblin realm is no place for a sprite such as you."

The queen's concern was contagious. It began to tickle over Lumina's skin.

"Is it so terrible?" she asked.

The soft brown ringlets bobbed as the queen nodded her head ever so slightly.

"I have never been, of course," she said. "We of the fairer folk are not welcome, but elementals come and go as they please. I have heard that darkness reigns there. That all is barren and dead, and there are no trees to whisper nor flowers to nod their pretty heads."

The concern tickling over Lumina's skin turned into a quiet terror, clinging to her like tree sap. An insidious thought came to her, of endless days trapped in such a place. With that thought came a certainty, which grew in her heart, until she knew beyond any doubt that if she were to go into the goblin city's she would never leave.

"Do not fret, little sister, do not fret," the Fairy Queen reached out and touched her shoulder again. "It is still possible that you could be freed from this fate."

"I cannot see how," Lumina said uncertainly. "Unless I break my oath and become forsworn."

"Perhaps there is another way," the queen said thoughtfully. "I might be able to help, but I need to know more. If you brought me something from the goblin's lands, a stone or some such thing, then I might be able to see how your fate could be changed. You will be free of this, I promise," the queen said reassuringly as she took up the boy's hand once again. "Look for us to come again in a fortnight."

With that, the Fairy Queen led the boy back the way

they had come. Above them the beech leaves glowed a translucent green in the sunlight, like peridots hanging from a lace of black branches. Their retreating heads were wreathed with halos of gold as they walked back through the sea of bluebells, to the hazel grove and doorway that would take them to Underhill.

As soon as they had gone, the silver cat stepped out from beneath the wild rose, coming to sit below the flower where Lumina still perched. He began licking his paw with great concentration, using it to wash first one ear, then the other.

"I don't trust her, Mistress," he said. "And neither should you."

"And who would you have me trust?" Lumina asked. The terror that she had felt a moment before had faded with the queen's departure, but had not gone away entirely.

"Me, of course," he answered, still washing his ears, "and the ones we have always trusted." Finished with his ablutions, he stood up and walked past her, rubbing his whiskered cheek along her foot.

"Don't worry, Mistress, everything will be fine," he said, disappearing into the tall grass once more.

She wandered restlessly through the meadow as the sky continued to darken, touching each leaf and petal she passed as if it would be for the last time. She wondered when she had begun to think that the Goblin King would not collect on her debt. Had, in fact, come to hope that he might not even know that a debt existed between them. Perhaps it was because Crow and Hoax had taken part in so much of the kitten's care. That they had stayed as a daily part of their lives even after the silver cat was able to fend for himself.

Worse yet, she could not stop the pang in her heart that came with the realization that the most likely way that the tale of her trespass would have reached the Goblin King's ears was from one of their lips.

As true night fell, a shaggy figure rose up from the lake. Neck arched and hooves flashing, the phooka danced merrily up to where Lumina was sitting, perched on a tall reed. He ended with a graceful genuflection at her feet, before springing up and shaking his pony head.

"Good evening, my fair fairy lass," he greeted her.

When she looked up at the phooka cavorting in front of her, he flinched away from her gaze, snorting in alarm.

"Ah, my Lady, sadness such as that was never meant for eyes such as yours," he said, stretching his softly fluttering nostrils towards her. "Tell me what I can do to take it away."

"May I ask a question, and you promise to answer it true?"

"I am your servant," he answered without hesitation. "Ask away."

She should not ask. She had no right to ask. But she knew if she did not, it would eat at her like a worm hidden in the heart of a perfect apple.

"I know that your fealty is to the Goblin King, as it should be, and that there is nothing owed me. But please tell me, was it you who told your king that I stole his tribute?" she asked, fearing the answer.

"No fairest," answered the phooka, gently. "I did not have to tell him, he already knew."

"Was it Crow then?" she asked, the words coming from her mouth before she could catch them.

"No, fairest," the phooka reassured her. "Crow did not have to tell the Goblin King."

The pain in her heart eased some at his answer, but it did nothing for the seed of fear that had begun growing there since the Fairy Queen's visit. It was beyond all reason, yet her limbs could not seem to stop trembling.

"There is something else troubling you, fairest," he pressed.

"Hoax, tell me about the goblin's kingdom," she forced the words out, despite the suffocating dread that had taken hold of her.

The phooka was silent.

"Let me show it to you, instead."

Lumina looked down to see Crow step out from beneath the broad leaves of a foxglove, the silver cat at his side.

"After all, words can mislead. It is better to see such things for yourself."

"Even for spirits such as us, the eyes can easily be deceived," she pointed out, the shaking in her voice making it hard for her to recognize it as her own.

The silver cat, purring madly, stretched his face up towards where she sat. The soft tickling of his whiskers on her foot caused her fear to take flight, chasing it away like mists before a bright morning sun.

"Perhaps," Crow agreed, "but the heart never can. Come down, my lady, share what I have brought with me.

Then if your curiosity outgrows your fear, I will take you to see the goblin city."

The goblin's presence, much like the silver cat's, was a balm to her troubled spirit. She acceded to his request, stepping from her perch to the top of the silver cat's head, before sliding down to join Crow on the ground.

And for a time, all was right in the world. She did not ask him where he had been, and he in turn, did not ask why she wished to see the goblin city. Instead they sat in companionable silence beneath a tangle of wood vetch that wound about cornflowers and heavy headed poppies, eating bread and honey as the night grew older about them.

The midnight hour came and went. A dark rainbow ringed the moon as she rode high above them now, pale and lovely in the velvety black sky. Her light shone softly down on the world below.

Lumina stood, and Crow did as well, coming up beside her as she looked out at the silver-washed land around them.

"Have you decided?" he asked her gently.

"I have," she answered just as softly.

"And do you wish me to take you to the goblin city?"

"I do," she said, sounding much surer than she felt. Or so she had thought, but Crow must not have been fooled because he took her hand in his.

"I can promise you this, my Lady of the Glade. You need only go as far as you wish, no further. My oath on it," he said. "And so I am bound, by the sun and the moon, the wind and the rain and by my own true name."

The oath, though made in all seriousness, brought a smile to Lumina's lips as she remembered when last he had made such an oath to her. With a lighter heart, she stepped out from the bower, still holding onto Crow's hand as she headed towards where she could hear the familiar banter between Hoax and the silver cat.

They left the glade a short time later, and were soon back among the wych-elm and oak of the Goblin Wood. The stygian darkness beneath their branches was absolute save where lances of moonlight pierced through the canopy above. The silver cat flitted alongside them like a ghost, occasionally disappearing into the gloom on his own errands, only to reappear later ahead of them.

Lumina and Crow sat shoulder to shoulder between the phooka's pointed pony ears. Throughout the whole of the day, Lumina had thought of an endless list of questions that she would ask Crow when next she saw him. But now that he was sitting right beside her, she could not bring herself to ask a single one.

But his arm was resting behind her, warm and solid, inviting her to lean against it. So she did, finding comfort in its familiarity despite all that had happened, or perhaps because of it.

They rode that way the night through, until the pale light of morning brought them to an old bridge, its ancient stones crumbling and covered in moss. In its many chinks and crannies small ferns and flowers grew.

Beneath it rushed a stream, foamy white, tumbling over large black boulders like a silver ribbon. Just beyond the bridge was a crossroads; a pale stone pillar stood to one side, spectral amongst the dark trees and darker earth. A cross, shaped so long ago that what it once was had been almost lost to the passing centuries.

They chose to stop there. The silver cat left them to their own devices as he went off to hunt for his breakfast. Hoax went off as well, to do whatever it is that phookas do to amuse themselves when there are no mortals around to trick. So that in the end, Lumina and Crow were the only ones left standing at the crossroads.

The first rays of the rising sun stretched their way through the trees, shining down along the path from which they had come until it fell on the pale stone cross, setting it aglow. A wondrous aldurescence drew Lumina closer. A shimmering blue, billowing amongst the shadows deep within the stone.

She came to the foot of the cross where a small font stood, filled with clear water. The stone was veined in black, just as the cross itself was. Rainbows chased themselves across its surface in some places; a dancing opalescence that niggled at her memory. She ran her hand along the font's rim as she walked along side its edge. The forget-me-nots growing around it whispered to her as she slipped through them.

"Moonstone," said Crow from somewhere above her.

Lumina looked up to where he sat atop a tumble of smaller stones that were piled up beneath the ancient monument. Whether they had been left when the cross had first been shaped or come to be there as it began to crumble, she did not know.

"The stone for your ring came from here," he said.

They had never spoken of the ring. In truth there had never been the chance to. A shyness stole over her. She reached out to stroke the flowers around her for comfort, running her fingers along their petals just as she would the silver cat's fur.

"What do your flowers tell you?" Crow asked softly.

"They speak of joy," she answered. "Joy, determination... and despair."

"Ah," he said, reaching down to pick up a pebble from the pile on which he sat. "I suppose that was to be expected."

"Is it? Lumina asked, as she sat down on the rim, dipping her fingers in the cold water. Light flashed brilliantly along the ripples she had set into motion. "Why would you expect them to know of such things?"

"Do you remember, at the Well of Stars when I told of the two lovers who would meet there?"

"I do," she said.

The memory of whispering trees and spinning stars set her skin atingle. Her toes curled as she remembered a dance that was like none other she had danced before. Crow watched her thoughtfully, his thumb caressing the stone he held in his hand. The idea that he might be thinking of that night as well flustered her; blushing, she looked back down at the diamonds on the water.

"She was a mortal woman and her lover was a fairy lord, a knight in the Queen's court," Lumina said.

"So they were. And the flowers and stones remember how they often met beneath the warm summer sun. She soon found that she was with child, as will often happen when two people meet and fall in love. And they were in love, so much so in fact that the fairy lord wished to stay with her and their child," Crow sighed. It sounded strange to Lumina's ears.

"So he did not leave her with empty promises or fairy gold that would only turn to autumn leaves with the morning light, as was usually done. Instead he told her how she could free him from the service he was bound to," Crow tossed the small pebble he had been holding into the very center of the font. It fell into the water with a quiet splash. "It was here, beneath this very cross that she did so, taking him beyond the Fairy Queen's power."

"And so the joy and determination is explained, but not the despair," said Lumina, brushing her hand across a forget-me-not's blue petal. "Was their end not a happy one?" she asked.

"Their end was a very happy one," Crow assured her. "But, when one person finds their happiness, it will often follow that another will find their despair."

There was a sadness to his words, a deep melancholy laced with a breath of bitterness, so at odds with this creature she had come to know so well. It made her heart stutter strangely to think what might make him sound so.

"This mortal woman," said Lumina, hesitating a little before continuing to ask. "Did you love her also?"

Crow looked at her for a moment with an expression she could not read, then suddenly he laughed and the air lightened.

"No, my Lady of the Glade. I was never Janet's lover and I can assure you that she never held my heart," he said, chuckling.

It was then that the silver cat returned, pushing his way through the flowers, licking his whiskers and looking very satisfied with himself.

Crow hopped gracefully down from his perch, coat-tails flaring as he landed just in front of Lumina.

"Well my Lady, shall we continue?" he asked, offering her his hand. She accepted without a second thought, slipping down from the font's edge.

"What of Hoax?" she asked.

"He knows where we are going, and if our friend is willing to carry us both then there is no need to wait for him," the goblin said, reaching up to stroke under the silver cat's chin who managed to look dignified and still purr madly. "Will you carry us my friend?"

"If I must," said the silver cat, although Lumina could tell that he did not mind at all.

Lumina vaulted to the silver cat's back. Crow followed up behind, his arms settling to either side of her. With his head resting just above hers, she felt as though he had wrapped her in his coat and tucked her into his chest. It was comforting. The same as when she nestled in with the silver cat. Though she doubted that she would ever tell him so.

The day was a strange one for Lumina. Never had she traveled so far from her glade. But she found that she was enjoying herself, even with the looming fear that came when she thought of what might await her at the journey's end.

Evening was falling when they came to a place where the oaks and elms had been replaced by a stand of soft-needled pines. There the silver cat stopped, informing them it was as far as he planned on going. Then he promptly curled up on the thick carpet of needles and fell asleep.

Lumina sat down next to him, leaning back against his shoulders as she often did. The wind sighed through the pines above them. The sound was much like the one she was used to hearing when they settled down to sleep beneath the wild rose's branches. However instead of one lone voice, it was a chorus of voices. The soft shushing sound was soothing, but it set her to wondering if Old Father Pine was ever lonely, standing all on his own as he did.

She had thought that perhaps Crow would come sit next to her, but he did not. Instead he surprised her by fashioning a fiddle from the needles at his feet and a few strands of the silver cat's fur. Twisting and shaping it as she had seen him do many times before, until it truly became what he willed it to be.

Without a word, he began to play for her. A sweet song of sleep, whose melody wrapped around her so subtlety that she never even knew that she had taken the step from the waking world to the land of dreams.

Crow set down his fiddle, leaving it to turn back into a few twists of pine needles woven through with silver fur as it left his hand. Turning from where the sprite lay sleeping, he made his way into the deep night shadows where Hoax stood waiting for him.

"I have left some things undone," he said to the phooka. "She will sleep till cock crow, but I will be back before then. Guard her well until I return."

Hoax snorted, "As if I would do anything else."

Crow waved a hand at him dismissively. "I will see you in the morning, my friend," he said, and with a shimmer he was gone.

Hoax shifted himself into a raven and flew up to perch on a pine branch far above the sleeping fairy.

"Lovely, lovely, Lumina... you have set such things in motion and do not even know it," he said to no one in particular. "I hope it brings him peace and not more despair. Sleep well, fairest." With a shake of his feathers he settled in for the night.

Below the silver cat opened one knowing eye.

When morning came, Lumina woke to a gray sky and warm brown bread. Where Crow, or perhaps it had been Hoax, had gotten it, no one said, and she did not ask, just accepted it gladly.

It came with a soft cheese which made the silver cat very happy. They sat on the thick carpet of needles, eating contentedly, as they watched the lowering clouds and listened to branches above them creak in the rising winds. Crow, his own breakfast finished, lay stretched out on his back, his hands behind his head as he looked up at the sky.

"We should be there by midday," he told her as she finished up the last crumbs of her breakfast.

"If it doesn't rain," said the silver cat, horn-eared and clearly unhappy with that particular possibility.

"Even if it does rain," Hoax said snorting softly at him, ruffling his fur. The silver cat flattened his ears and looked at the phooka with open disdain.

"Stop teasing him, Hoax," Lumina admonished.

"As you wish, lady mine," said the phooka, tossing his forelock rakishly at her. A bit of mischief still glinted in his eyes.

Crow snorted softly, rolling effortlessly to his feet.

"It might be best if we don't give that one a chance to think of more ways to entertain himself. If you are ready..." he said, holding his hand out to her, which she took by way of assent. "Let us be on our way then."

So Lumina and Crow set off as they had the night before, riding between the phooka's pointy ears. But this time Hoax also carried the silver cat perched imperiously on his broad rump. The shushing of the pines rose with the winds; dry needles skittered across the ground and the sylphs gathered them up, twisting them into small wind devils and set them swirling just ahead of the phooka's hooves.

Eventually the trees came to an end. They stepped out from beneath the forest's eaves onto a vast moorland. The sun overhead was hidden behind a heavy blanket of clouds. The sylphs rode the wild winds that whipped around them, shrieking joyously as they raced ahead across the budding heather; returning occasionally to tug on the cat's whiskers or kiss Lumina on the cheek.

The land changed as they continued on beneath the lowering sky, the earth's skin becoming thinner and thinner until its ancient bones pushed clear through.

Rounding the edge of a hillock, they came upon a long lake. It lay twisting at the foot of the dark hills, a silvered mirror reflecting the slate-colored clouds above them.

The phooka carried them along the water's edge, out onto a barren spit of land where stood the ruins of an old keep. He passed through the gate, coming to the foot of some steps which lay just beyond. That is where he left his passengers, to make their way up to the battlements above.

Crow led them up the steps, and upon reaching their end continued on, leaping to the top of the stone parapet. Lumina followed, the silver cat close behind her.

The wind which had been blocked by the ruin's decaying walls found them once again. It laid the silver cat's whiskers flat and set Crow's coattails to flapping. Lumina felt the tug and pull of her hair. The wind twined it about her like a living thing, the world appearing in flashes between its midnight blue strands.

To one side of her, far below, lay the lake. On the other was the keep's bailey, choked with weeds and stones that had fallen from the walls and towers surrounding it. It was an empty, crumbling keep in a barren, desolate kingdom. But it was hardly one of eternal darkness as the Fairy Queen had warned.

"Is this the Goblin King's keep?" she asked as they continued along the parapet, leaping from merlon to merlon across the open crenels.

"Yes... and no," Crow answered.

Lumina laughed, despite herself.

"As straight an answer as ever Hoax has given me," she said.

Crow scoffed.

"And yet that is the best answer I can give you, nonetheless," he assured her. "The truth of it will be made clear up ahead."

The battlements, of which the parapet they had been following was only a part, ended at the side of an old watchtower. There stood a doorway. Contained within its frame was a blackness, a yawning void drawing in the light, but giving nothing back.

"If there are truths here, I do not see them," she said, her eyes sliding away from the absolute darkness that filled the doorway.

"Come, I will show you," Crow said, beckoning her to his side with a graceful sweep of his arm.

She went to stand with him at the merlon's edge, where it looked out over the lake. It lay unnaturally still, despite the winds racing across its surface. A perfect mirror for the roiling clouds above.

"Look," he said, nodding to the unwavering water below.

Lumina looked down at the reflection of the ruined keep. A broad lance of sunlight pierced the clouds above, as if it had been waiting for just that moment. Lumina looked up at the golden pathway now falling across the hills, cutting an emerald swath along their dark flanks, before finally coming to rest on the lake itself.

"Look again," said Crow, his hand settling on her shoulder as he pointed once more to the water below.

When she did, she found that the reflection in the water was no longer that of a crumbling ruin, but of a great stone keep, whole and proud.

"Turn around, fair one," Crow said, his taloned hand gently turning her back towards the keep on which they stood.

The same crumbling ruin greeted her, but the doorway was no longer filled with a crushing darkness. Instead it opened on to a busy market. Goblins of all kinds wandered through the stalls: bucca, brownies and barguest. Here a gruagach, there a hogboon; she even saw a human or two browsing amongst the merchants' wares.

Just beyond the sprawling market place was what she guessed to be the Goblin King's Keep. It looked much as the reflection in the lake had, save the walls and towers were black as night. Long banners of a silver stag, leaping across a crimson field, hung from its battlements.

"Do you wish to go in?" Crow asked. He had leaned in close and his breath was warm on her ear.

The fear which had been gone most of the day returned a hundredfold. Those who wandered the marketplace now appeared frenzied and desperate to her eyes. The Keep loomed above them ominously, its banners pulsing like open wounds on its flanks.

"No," she said shaking her head vehemently. "No, I don't think so," she said again, stepping back a little. Her back unexpectedly came up against the solid warmth that was Crow. Much to her surprise, reassuring arms held her close for a moment before letting her go.

"And there is no need for you to do so, if you do not wish to," he assured her.

The sun disappeared behind the clouds, as if it had been waiting for permission. Likewise the goblin market was gone, blackness filling the doorway once more.

Lumina turned away. Sinking down until she was sitting with her legs dangling over the merlon's edge, she looked out over the lake's mirrored surface. Crow sat next to her.

"What is wrong, fairest?" he asked. "Why did you wish to come here only to stop at the gate?"

She wanted to confide in him all of her fears; to ask about what the Fairy Queen had told her, but her lips refused to move. Her tongue remained still, frozen to the roof of her mouth, and she could not utter a word. However, when she rested her hands to either side of her, a small pebble found its way into her palm. Without thinking, she placed it in her spider-silk bag.

Crow's sharp eyes watched her closely as the silence drew out. Then he took one of her hands and stood, gently pulling her up as well. He studied her face with what she thought might be concern, though with him it was often hard to tell. Still she could not bring herself to tell him the fear that was foremost in her thoughts.

Finally he nodded to himself, tucking her hand into the crook of his arm.

"If we are done here then there is a place I believe

we should go and a person you should meet," he said, leading her back towards where the silver cat waited, tail twitching.

The silver cat carried them back down from the ruined battlements to where Hoax stood just beyond the gate, dripping wet and covered with water weed. Not a surprising state for a phooka who had been left too long to his own devices.

"I had wondered if you would ever return," he said, shaking his dripping mass of a mane.

"I think, perhaps, that it would be better if we stayed where we are," Crow said. "Do you agree, lady?"

Lumina smiled. "Oh, yes, wholeheartedly!"

"Hoax, make yourself useful then and fly ahead. Tell her we will be there before nightfall," said Crow.

The phooka snorted. "As you command," he said. Shaking himself all over, he changed into a raven and took to the air. Circling, he dipped over them once, then set off roughly in the direction from which they had come.

"Who is to expect us before nightfall?" Lumina asked the goblin sitting behind her.

"A friend whom I hope you will like," he answered.

"Of course she will like her," the silver cat said. "After all, I like her."

CHAPTER 7

Cats Do Love
Their Secrets

The silver cat carried them back up onto the wind-swept moors. The way he chose was not quite the same as the way they had come. But he set out with a surety that made Lumina wonder just how often he came to visit the Goblin King's domain.

The distance they traveled back may have been shorter, but the journey took longer. Evening was falling as they came down off the heather-covered moorlands. The wood rose abruptly before them. There at its edge was a narrow path which the silver cat followed. It led them only a short ways into the whispering pines before coming to an end in front of a small cottage. Ivy grew up its stone walls and its roof was covered with sod. Diamond-paned windows of colored glass glowed like gems in the gathering gloom, as golden light spilled from a door that had been left open to the evening air.

The little house and its garden were surrounded by a dense gorse hedge. Curiously enough, innumerable bells hung throughout it, bells of brass and silver, iron and glass, all shining amongst the flowering branches. Their chiming was only mildly unpleasant to Lumina's ears, at first. But as they drew closer, the ringing grew more and more maddening; a discordant noise that was like needles under her skin. She was about to tell the silver cat to stop when Crow leaned in close behind her, speaking softly next to her ear.

"Bide a while," he urged, reaching his long arm around her to cover her hand with his own. "There is a formality to be observed, and then it will subside."

The hedge was broken by an iron-bound wooden gate, beside which stood two thorn trees, heavy with berries just starting to blush. There, the silver cat stopped, pausing for just a moment as though he expected the gate to open itself. When it didn't, he meowed loudly and none too patiently.

The figure of a woman soon appeared in the doorway. Her hair was streaked with silver but her back unbent by age. She walked to the gate where the silver cat and his passengers waited, stopping in the shadow of the thorn trees' branches.

"Good evening, eld woman," Crow greeted her.

"Good evening. Hoax said that you would be along," said the eld woman, bowing her head slightly in their direction. "And, I see another who visits me often enough, whenever he wants a bowl of cream. But I do not know the last of your companions," she said, not unkindly.

"But you have heard of her," Crow said mildly, almost teasingly.

"Ah, of course, your Lady of the Glade. I am happy to finally meet you," the eld woman said. "Enter my gate and be welcome from now until the sun sets tomorrow."

The maddening sound of the bells subsided at the eld woman's words, becoming only a soothing lullaby on the night wind.

She beckoned to them, turning back towards the house. The silver cat followed her out of the soft darkness. The golden light of the eld woman's house reached out to welcome them, carrying with it the scent of the drying herbs and steeping tea.

Crow saw Lumina settled in. Then, much to her surprise, he left, taking Hoax with him, and leaving her with the promise that they would return by morning.

So now she found herself sitting on a sachet of roses and sweet marjoram, atop the eld woman's kitchen table, a small blue thimble filled with warm tea in her hands. Across from her sat the eld woman. A porcelain cup, thin and delicate as a seashell, rested on a saucer in front of her. On the table between them was a teapot to match, fragrant steam spiraling up from its spout.

Lumina knew little of human homes. Though the outside of the house had been plain, with its stone walls and sod roof, the inside sparkled like a queen's bower, baubles and curiosities winking everywhere in the soft light of the hearth. Flowering vines were painted along the soft green walls in vibrant hues, gold flashing at the edge of every leaf and petal. She felt strangely comfortable, as if she had been there many times before. Perhaps it was because of the silver cat who, having finished his bowl of cream long ago, lay curled up on the hearth rug in front of the warm fire.

The eld woman smiled at her as she offered to add a drop of honey to Lumina's tea. Thin crow's feet swept out from the corners of her eyes, in an otherwise smooth face. Her eyes, one dark gray with tiny flecks running through it like molten silver; the other, paler gray and clouded like a stormy sky; watched her with obvious good humor.

"Do you like the tea?" she asked Lumina.

"It is delicious," Lumina said, sipping again from her thimble. "It was kind of you to offer us your hospitality, especially given that we were somewhat thrust upon you. Although, the silver cat seems to be a frequent visitor."

"Yes," said the eld woman, turning to look at the sleeping cat fondly. "He does come to see me often. And has done, since he was just out of kittenhood. Oh, he was so lanky and awkward then! I believe that he was just learning to hunt and wasn't always that successful... not that he would ever admit such."

Lumina smiled, remembering that time well. "He did think himself the stealthiest of creatures back then, didn't he! It amused the Rowan Maiden's birds so much that they used to pretend not to see him, even when he was hiding in plain sight. That was, until he actually managed to snatch a redwing's tail feathers. Then they scolded him for days!"

The eld woman laughed. "He never told me that! Though he has said a great deal about you."

"Has he now!" said Lumina with a touch of surprise, though she vaguely remembered as much from their meeting at the garden gate. "I am afraid he has neglected to tell me anything of you," she admitted, turning her annoyed gaze towards the blissfully unaware, and most likely uncaring, silver cat.

The corners of the woman's eyes crinkled further. "Cats do love their secrets!" she said merrily. "Just like the fae."

They spoke long into the night and found they had at least two things in common: their fondness for growing things and a shared love of the incorrigible silver cat. So, it was late when the eld woman finally sought her bed, and Lumina found herself sitting on the sill of an open window. She leaned against the casement looking out into the night-shrouded garden.

She had enjoyed the eld woman's company very much and was glad to have met her. But, she did not understand why Crow and Hoax had not stayed. She might have even felt abandoned, had her hostess not been so pleasant, and had the silver cat not seemed so obviously at home in the eld woman's house.

Other creatures' comings and goings was not something she usually took note of, save for the silver cat, and now it would seem her two goblins as well.

She pondered this as she listened to the soft chime of the hedge bells, watching the crescent moon drift through the night sky, a fine-spun boat of pearl on a quiet sea of stars.

Sleep must have eventually come to her because the morning was already well and begun when Lumina awoke. She opened her eyes to its golden light washing over her and Crow, who was asleep, propped up next to her on the casement. She studied him with heavy-lidded eyes as the honeyed light dusted his obsidian beak in gold and set the dark rainbows dancing over his feathers. She reached out her hand to smooth them.

"Leave him be, fairest," said a familiar voice from just outside the window. "It's rare when he sleeps so peacefully."

She lowered her hand reluctantly, looking out from where she sat to the garden beyond. There was Hoax, perched on the edge of a shallow stone basin filled with water.

"You should come join me, instead," he continued, stepping into the basin where he began to clean his feathers. "The water is cold and sweet." He punctuated this by flicking water into the air where it flashed like diamonds as it fell.

She heard the silver cat grumble at this statement. He was sitting under the broad leaves of a foxglove not far away. Though far enough away, to be safe from the phooka's exuberant splashing. The eld woman was further out in the garden, walking along the narrow paths with clouds of butterflies as her attendants. Lumina decided to leave the phooka and cat to their own devices in favor of joining the eld woman as she went about gathering her herbs.

It was almost noon when Crow joined them. The eld woman set out berries and cream, which they ate happily as they whiled away the day in good company, taking their leave only when the sun began to set.

The eld woman bid them farewell at her garden gate. To Lumina, she gave a curious gift. A golden bell no bigger than a grain of wheat; its clapper tied up tight with red thread.

"My bells shouldn't be a bother to you now," said the eld woman. "Know that you are welcome here whenever you want to visit."

With that she wished them a fair journey, making it known to the silver cat that he should bring his mistress with him when next he came to call.

The measure of peace that Lumina had found left her as they departed from the house at the edge of the wood. In its absence, the vague feeling of unease that had come with the Fairy Queen's warnings returned, more noticeable now after its absence. Yet the feeling faded quickly, and with it, any desire to talk about it faded as well.

They traveled the night through, coming to the border stream at dawn. There they parted company with Crow's promise to see them soon. The silver cat carried her across the ford and on towards home, where they promptly curled up in the first pool of sunlight they found, and fell fast asleep.

Lumina slept the day away, not waking till late in the afternoon. Which, in and of itself, was not really a surprise; unlike the being she saw standing at the edge of her glade when she awoke.

The white stag was there just beyond the trees' shadow, bathed in brilliant light. He was a sight to behold with his pale coat sparkling beneath the sun's caress.

He must have been waiting for her to wake, because as soon as she saw him he started towards her. Even beneath the dimness of the trees he was magnificent, glowing like the moon at her zenith as he made his way through the glade to where Lumina was. Stopping at a respectful distance, he lowered his head to regard them with his moonstone eyes.

"Goblin King," she said, standing at his approach and offering him a curtsy. "You were not expected."

Puzzlement filled his pale eyes for a moment, but then he slowly nodded.

"Perhaps I should have sent a messenger ahead," he said and Lumina worried that it had not been puzzlement, but offense that she had seen in his face. She hastened to make amends.

"It is not to say that you are not welcome," she assured him, although her statement was just on the edge of truthfulness.

A whisper of whiskers tickled her arm as the silver cat passed her, boldly walking up to the white stag.

"No cream, no fish, no cheese?" he said as he rubbed his head along the stag's jaw, his tail curling impudently over the elegant muzzle as he did so. "Then why did you come to see me?"

"I did not come to see you, you impertinent thing. I came to see your mistress," the white stag retorted. "Good afternoon, lady. I realize my coming was unexpected but I was hoping that you would join me for a few hours."

"You wish to spend time with me?" she asked, a bit alarmed at such an idea. "To what end?"

"To what end," he chuckled, leaning even closer as he did so. Soft breath whispered over her, cool and fresh like the air just before a storm. "Because I wish to court you. As I said before, I would rather it was the price of your heart, not the price of your debt that brings you to me on our wedding day."

Lumina found her heart pounding at the thought, but whether it was with anticipation or terror she could not say.

"And I have things I would share with you. Things you might find of interest," said the white stag, retreating a little. "Come with me, fair one, and I promise that you will be as safe as if you had never left your glade."

"And will you return me to my glade?" she asked, with more confidence than she felt.

The white stag nodded his head. "My oath in it, before the church bells finish tolling the midnight hour."

The silver cat gave a little sneeze. "Well... then... there is no reason for me to go," he said.

"What do you mean, Dearest?" Lumina asked, more than a little unnerved at the thought of being alone with the Goblin King, even in his guise as the white stag, which was admittedly less intimidating.

"No cream, no milk, no fish, no reason for me to go," he said, sitting down to wash his ears. "But don't worry about me, Mistress," the silver cat said, pausing to look at Lumina with big round eyes. He blinked once, slowly; the picture of cat innocence.

"My Lady, I would be happy to carry you," the white stag said soothingly, tilting his proud head so that she might easily sit on his antler if she chose to. And so she did, somewhat hesitantly, glancing at her treacherous companion, who only blinked innocently at her again.

She wrapped her arm around the burnished silver brow tine as the stag lifted his head smoothly.

"I will see you soon, Dearest," Lumina called back as the stag stepped out into the late afternoon light. The silver cat closed his eyes tight, giving her a knowing cat smile, before going back to his washing.

The white stag set off towards Serene's lake, in nearly the opposite direction from the one which Lumina expected him to go.

They glided over the ground as though it was the wind's back she rode on, for it seemed as though the stag's hooves never touched the earth. He did not slow at the lake's edge, stepping out over the water without a pause. Each silver hoof touched down lightly on first one lily pad, then another, and another as though they were merely mist drifting across the lake's sparkling face. They came to the far shore with nary a ripple of its bright surface.

On he went, over the lands beyond until they came to a sleepy stream. There he turned, following it as it meandered over grassy meadows. The crystalline waters flowing quietly over large rounded pebbles struck Lumina as familiar. A memory came to her of the first night she had met Crow. Of being carried along by the lazy waters, on a shell full of goat's milk.

She had been elated, terrified and very unsure of how she was to take care of her newfound kitten. A growing warmth filled her heart. No matter that she was currently riding on the antlers of the very creature whose tribute she had stolen that night.

She began to wonder about their course, and perhaps to worry just a little, when she noticed small shapes moving in the distance. The White Stag must have seen them as well. He stopped, the long grass rippling around them in the wind.

"Here comes the first thing I wished to show you; a gift, if it pleases you. Though truth be told, it is more for the boy than for yourself. I understand he comes to visit you?" he asked.

"He does," she answered, a touch of wariness in her voice.

The White Stag chuckled. "No harm to him, I swear, perhaps even some good. Hold on, my blue rose," he said, then leapt.

His first leap brought her close enough to see that the shape was that of a nanny goat ambling along with her head down. With the second, she could see that the nanny goat was not alone. The third brought them closer still, enough so that Lumina could see the nanny goat was the same one whom she had met at the farmhouse the year before. The very one who had given her a ride to the milking shed, so that she could find food for her kitten.

There they stopped, waiting as the strange procession headed towards them.

The nanny goat paid them no mind as she ambled closer, too intent on a choice bit of grass that continued to stay just out of her reach. The clump of sod always moving just as the nanny was about to nibble at the tantalizingly green shoots. The goat tried again, and again the bit of grass moved, on what Lumina could now see were a pair small spindly legs. A goblin's face peaked out from beneath, smiling cheekily and winking at her.

The rest of the troupe was made of piskies, and bogies, and other such goblins happily dancing around, under and over the old nanny goat. And on her back sat a gruagach. She was the size of a small child and brown as a nut. The only clothing she wore was her long hair which was leaf green and covered her completely. Hopping down from her seat, she made her way over to where the white stag waited.

"Master," she said, bobbing in a quick curtsy.

"Meg," the White Stag acknowledged.

"We should be at the glade by nightfall," she assured him. "We left a phooka in the nanny's stead, so none will miss her. Last we saw, he was leading the herdboy a merry chase, but he will be away by dawn with no one the wiser."

"You've done well," the stag said nodding his head slightly.

Seeming to take that as a dismissal, Meg bobbed quickly to him once again, and returned to her charge, hopping neatly back up onto the old goat's back.

The merry band passed them by, heading in the direction from which Lumina had just come.

"They are bringing her to the glade? My glade?" Lumina asked, as the stag moved off in a direction that took them away from the little procession.

"Yes, my lady. Unless you say otherwise," he answered. "For when the boy visits. I thought it would be good if he could have fresh milk when next he came to your glade. I know how it is under the fairy hill; the food has little substance for a mortal soul."

"But I know nothing of milking goats," said Lumina, wondering what she would do with such a creature.

"No fear, sweet sprite. Meg will milk her, care for her and make sure no harm comes to her," he assured Lumina, continuing on over the sighing grass towards the shadowed wood.

The sun sat low on the horizon as they passed beneath the eaves of the Goblin Wood. Spears of its rosy brilliance followed them into the trees, only to be swallowed up by the eternal twilight that reigned there. The white stag shivered all over, as if shaking off flies. His step seemed to become even lighter, if that were at all possible.

"There are no prying eyes for us to worry about here," he said. "Nor ears either, so we can speak freely."

"And what would those prying ears be likely to hear?" Lumina asked.

"A story, nothing more," replied the stag. "A story that I think it only right that you should know, since now you have become a part of it. The telling of it will not be short, but I hope that you will be willing to hear it."

"I am," she said. "It would be foolish of me not to, no matter the length of it."

"True enough," agreed the White Stag. "Well I suppose the beginning is the best place to start. You see, all these lands were once ruled over by a mortal lord. He was a good man, who had to his credit two fine sons, whose mother was famed for her cleverness and beauty. Unearthly beauty, some would say, And they would be right, for she had without a doubt come from the land of Faerie. Sadly, she disappeared shortly after the birth of their second son. Their father became lost in grief, retreating from the cares of the world, leaving the raising of his sons to their grandfather."

They came to a clearing in the woods. In the center stood a rath, covered in short grass and primroses but nothing else. In an easy leap the white stag carried them to the top of it.

"The lord's sons eventually grew into young men, well regarded by those around them. They often rode out with their grandfather, who had a great love for the hunt, and that was how the Fairy Queen first saw them. She thought them beautiful, so she spirited them both away, from the very mound we stand on, no less. They went to live with her, in Underhill, and for seven years they served the Fairy Queen in her court.

"They would come to find out later that more than a hundred years had passed in the mortal world, and that all they knew had gone to dust. At first it mattered little to them. They loved the Fairy Queen, holding her above all else. And she, in turn, loved them because they were new and lovely and full of life."

A sigh escaped the white stag, "But for mortals, or those who once were, such things are not always enough. The loss of all he once knew preyed heavily on the mind of the younger brother. So he took to walking in the mortal realm more and more."

He leapt down from where they stood, heading back into the woods' embrace. True night was falling, and baobhan sith were dancing between the tree's gnarled trunks, while the ghosts of dead men wandered by them. But Lumina had no fear of either, having never been mortal.

They stepped from the darkness into a well of moonlight shining down on a familiar clearing of forget-me-nots. Silver-washed roses nodded their sleepy heads over crumbling stones. A strange ache bloomed in her heart.

Magic slid over her skin like a soft rain. In its wake she found herself no longer perched in the white stag's antlers, but standing hand in hand with the Goblin King. The clearing seemed much smaller now. The crumbling walls of the well where once she danced, now a narrow ring of stones just wide enough to sit on.

"Why are we here?" she asked, as they made their way to its edge.

The Goblin King did not answer her, reaching out instead to thoughtfully stroke his long fingers over the rose's soft petals. It brought to mind the story that Crow had told her when last they were here, and she wondered if the Goblin King also could hear the secrets the roses whispered.

"Do the roses speak to you, Goblin King?" she asked, curious as to what his answer would be and hopeful that he would continue the story he had been telling.

"No, sweet sprite, not as they do for you. But if I could hear them, I'm sure they would tell me of a wandering fairy lord and the mortal woman he met in this very spot, one Midsummer's Eve. No doubt they would sing of the love that grew between them."

The roses' whispers grew louder as the Goblin King's story took on a familiar ring and Lumina wondered if she would hear the whole telling of the tale that Crow had only hinted at.

"It must have been a great love for the flowers to whisper of it still," she said.

"It was," agreed the Goblin King. "So much so that the younger brother decided to leave Faerie, and return to the mortal realm so that he could be with her. But, he was bound in service to the Fairy Queen. Despite the danger that it would entail, he told his lover how she could free him."

"So on Hollentide Eve, the woman waited at the cross-roads for the fairy host to ride by, her lover with them. She let pass the black horse and the brown, but when the milk-white steed made to ride by her, she rushed up and pulled the rider from his back. She held fast and endured all the trials her lover had warned her of, until at last, she had freed him from his service."

"As for the eldest brother, he too had been with the host. Astride the black horse, he had ridden by the mortal woman without taking notice. And he was at the side of the Fairy Queen when his brother was freed from her ser-vice; he listened to her curse his brother, wishing that she had plucked the eyes from his head, and replaced them with ones of stone. She raged because the youngest broth-er was beyond her reach. The eldest, however, was not. In her anger, she plucked the eyes from his head, giving him ones of moonstone in their stead. She turned him into a moon-white stag and banished him from her court, setting her Hunt to hound his footsteps. She did this all believing he had known of the two lovers, which indeed he had. Though he had not known of all their plans."

The memory of a story Crow had told her that past winter flared bright in her mind, bringing understanding with it in brilliant clarity. She looked up into the Goblin King's pale eyes.

"You were the eldest brother?" she said.

"Yes," he said, "and for a hundred years I fled the Queen's hounds. My only saving grace, a loyal servant who offered to share in my exile. He rode on my antlers and for all the time that we traveled together through these woods, he was my eyes. Perhaps we would still be as we were then, if not for an unexpected kindness that gave me back my sight, if not my eyes. Stone eyes the queen gave me, and now stone they will always be."

Lumina did not know what to say, so she reached out and took his hand.

"Ah, do not look at me so, my light. Eyes such as yours were not made for such sadness," he said, smiling gently at her as he stroked the backs of his elegant fingers down her cheek.

"Unlike yourself, the Fairy Queen is capricious by nature. Her anger, like her love, is fleeting. She had soon forgotten what she had done and the passion that had driven her to do it. She searched out the white stag, believing that he might return to her court only to find that he now had a kingdom and a court of his own and no desire to return to hers. So she believed herself betrayed yet again. But like my brother, I was now beyond her reach. I had gathered all that she had left unnoticed and built my kingdom in a place that had long been tied to the blood of my family."

"And what of your brother? Did you ever speak to him again?" Lumina asked. "Did he know what fate you had suffered?"

"No, he did not," the Goblin King said, his answer held only the slightest touch of bitterness. "He married Janet, and they lived long and happily together. However she, being mortal, eventually died, which was something he could no longer do. For though he had been mortal once, he had been too long in the fairy realm, and being half-fae himself such a stay had changed him. Still, his love was great enough that he found a way to follow her through death's black door. Their descendants continue to live at the edge of the fairies' wood; in a great manor house that was Janet's family home. They had been taught not to go into the wood. But that was a long time ago and mortal memories are as short as mortal lives. So a young boy, beautiful and golden and very much like his many greats-grand sire, chased a pretty bubble to someplace he should not have gone and the Fairy Queen spirited him away. Which finally brings us, sweet sprite, to where your part in the story begins."

Lumina could not be sure, but it seemed that the smile he gave her was edged with regret.

"I had heard that a mortal boy had been brought to the Queen's court and that he looked much as my brother once had. So, when the Fairy Queen invited me to join her for the Midsummer revel, I accepted, as she knew I would. And she made sure I saw the boy, but that he was beyond my reach. If I could not touch him, then I could not determine if he was, in truth, blood kin to me. She also knew I would feel obligated to ask for him, just on the chance that he was what she claimed him to be, and that I would be cornered into accepting whatever conditions she set. Which, as it turned out, was for me to take a bride from her court."

He sighed, "From there I am not sure of her plan. Perhaps all would have refused me, and she would have had her revenge for my refusal to return to her. Or perhaps, only the one she had chosen would have accepted my proposal, which itself would have been an insult, for all that were dancing widdershins that night were the cruelest and most uncouth of her court."

"However," he said smiling at Lumina in the most wolfish sort of way, "she did not consider those of you who danced in the direction of the sun to be any I would choose from. For she certainly would not have. Or perhaps she believed all of you would return whence you came when your masks were removed. Truth be told, I am of a mind that she did not think of you at all, giving you no more thought than she would have butterflies at the edge of a meadow. And of course she knew nothing of your debt to me. Believe me when I say that if she had, she would have gone to any length to make sure you did not attend."

Lumina looked away then, biting her tongue for fear

she would ask how he had known of her debt, not wanting to hear what answer he would give.

Instead she asked, "How did you know me?"

"The silver cat, of course," he answered, a smile edging his words. "He knows me quite well."

Now it was her turn to sigh. The eld woman had been right, cats do love their secrets.

The Goblin King took both of her hands in his own, drawing her attention back to him. Capturing her eyes with his own, luminous in the moonlight as they looked down at her almost sadly.

"Lumina, there is a way out of this for you," he said. "If the boy is not of my blood, then I have no obligation to protect him, and you will be free of your own obligation to me."

"You would not save him if he were not of your blood?" she asked, her heart tightening at the thought of the boy staying as he was.

"Would you still want me to?" he asked, and there was such an intensity in his gaze that her breath froze in her breast.

"Yes," she finally answered. "I would not want him to stay as he is."

"Then save him we will," he said. "The Queen brings him to see you, does she not?" Lumina nodded and he continued. "Bring me a few drops of his blood if you can, so that I can determine for myself if he is of my brother's line or not. If he is, it may be easier to help him. Can you do that?"

"Yes," she answered, her reluctance plain.

"I promise that I mean no harm to the boy," he reassured her. "Now, it is almost midnight, and if I am not to be forsworn then we should head back."

With that he became the white stag once again, Lumina sitting amongst his silver antlers.

As he carried her towards home, she considered his story. There was no doubt of its truth, for it had been straight forward and plain in its telling. His company had been pleasant and he had shown concern for the boy and a thought for his care. It made her wonder if it would be so bad to be his bride, that perhaps the Goblin King's Keep was not as the Fairy Queen had feared. After all, she had admitted to having never seen it for herself. And the Goblin King had done no wrong to Lumina save for calling in a debt, rightfully owed to him. And, more telling than all the rest, at least in her eyes, the silver cat liked him. Perhaps she should speak to Crow about him. A sad reluctance came over her, as it always did when she thought of Crow and her wedding. She decided against mentioning it to him.

It was just before midnight when they reached the stream which served as the border between her glade and the goblin's wood. At the water's edge, Lumina found herself once again hand in hand with the Goblin King.

"My Lady, I have a small request," he said, leaning in so that the only thing she could see was his bewitchingly handsome face; his long star-white hair falling like silk over their clasped hands. "When you have gotten what I have asked for, will you bring it to me in my Keep?"

Uncertainty and a quiet terror seized her as it always did whenever she thought of going to the Goblin Keep. It set her hands to trembling.

He must have felt it for his eyes filled with concern.

"What do you fear, my lady?" he asked gently. But as it had been at the ruins, she could not speak of her fear; her fear that she would be bound forever if she was ever to go to his keep.

He stayed where he was for the longest time, watching her with knowing eyes.

"I promise you, my light, there is no reason for you to fear me. I will never keep you where you do not wish to be kept, not now and not if we wed. My oath bind me to this, by the sun and the moon, the wind and the rain and by my own true name."

To Lumina, it was as if this night had been transposed with another, and it was Crow standing before her, making a similar oath. The words shattered whatever spell had been laid on her. The terror vanished like shadows before the dawning sun, making Lumina wonder about what power the Fairy Queen's words might have held over her.

She smiled brilliantly at the goblin man standing in front of her, only to have it quickly fade at the realization that the eyes she was gazing into were of moonstone, not obsidian. For just a moment, she had forgotten that it was not Crow standing with her. She drew back her hands, confused by the tricks her mind had played.

"Will you come to my keep, when you have what I have asked for?" the Goblin King asked again, and she noticed that he had not mentioned the boy's blood directly since leaving his domain. She understood, nonetheless.

"Perhaps," she answered noncommittally, no longer feeling the need to stay away, but not feeling a need to go either.

"I understand," he said. "In your own good time, sweet sprite."

A flock of birds spiraled from out of the night sky, the king's knights most likely. They flew steadily over the stream, making a bridge of their backs for them to cross. There on the far shore sat the silver cat, tail about his paws, waiting as if he had been in that very same spot all night.

"It is midnight," he pointed out.

"Only just," she said. "Were you worried?"

"No," the silver cat said, but the tip of his tail twitched once, hard.

Lumina stepped away from the Goblin King, her hand leaving his as she did so. Between one step and the next she was tiny again. She walked up to the silver cat. He lowered his head so that she could wrap her arms around it as far as they would go, burying her face in his warm furry cheek. He began to purr softly.

The fluttering of wings made her look back over her shoulder. The Goblin King was again a white stag, luminescent in the moon's light, a host of birds wheeling above his burnished silver antlers.

"Good night, my lady. Rest well," was all he said, and with that, the Goblin King and his host headed out into the night.

Exactly one fortnight from their last visit, the Fairy Queen brought the boy back to Lumina's glade, as promised.

They arrived the same way as they had before, walking hand in hand through the sea of bluebells, the Fairy Queen in her guise of a sweet-cheeked little girl, and the boy, beautiful, golden and more than a little mad.

Lumina greeted them excitedly, telling the Fairy Queen that she wished to show the boy all around. Taking the boy's hand, she urged him to follow her. He seemed to glow with health, but his finger felt skeletal, giving truth to the lie. And she now better understood what the Goblin King had meant when he said that the food of faerie held little substance for a mortal.

Skipping from grass top to grass top, she was able to keep hold of the boy's finger while she led him along, the queen trailing behind them. Lumina led them from the glade, to the meadow, to the lake where the waters shimmered bright in the morning light, in the hopes that the queen might grow bored of their wandering. And so she did, leaving Lumina and the boy to continue on while she stayed on the lake's sandy shore, trailing her fingers in the water so that little silvery fish could nibble at them.

Lumina led the boy back to the glade, to a blackberry bramble where she fed him the choicest fruits. Further into the wood where the hazel grew; there she gave him nuts that she had imbued with peace and vitality, while Meg brought him fresh milk in clever little birch bark cups. He ate them dutifully but with little enthusiasm, his eyes still staring through her to a world that only he could see. But at least he stopped breaking out into mad laughter, which gave Lumina hope.

They ended their ramble at the wild rose, where she bade him pick a rosehip, ripe and red, from deep in the tangle of stems. As he did so the rose reached out and pricked the boy's finger as Lumina had asked it to do, drinking in the drops of blood and holding them for her.

The boy's eyes cleared then, looking straight at her for the first time. A crystal tear welled up, falling down his smooth cheek.

"There, there sweetling, don't cry," Lumina said, reaching out from her perch on the rose to pat his cheek. "It will only be a little longer, then all will be well," she promised.

With her hand on his finger, she led him away, back towards the meadow where the queen joined them once more. As soon as the Fairy Queen took the boy's hand, the dreamy smile returned.

They stayed the rest of the afternoon, but if the queen noticed the scratches on the boy's arms she never mentioned it.

The sky was purple with the coming twilight when the Fairy Queen finally made as if to leave. Taking up the boy's hand, she turned to Lumina. Her child's eyes were strangely lucent in the deepening dusk.

"One more thing little sister," she said in her sweet piping voice. "Have you managed to get what I asked for?"

Lumina had handed the stone she had taken from the battlements over to the queen before even realizing she had taken it from her spider silk bag. The queen smiled at her.

"It is perfect," she said, as Lumina stared in disbelief at the minuscule pebble resting in the child-size hand. "Well done, little sister. Well done."

Lumina wondered what she had done as she watched the Fairy Queen leave with the boy, back through the dark trunks of the trees, the will'o wisps floating overhead, dead men's candles to light the way.

CHAPTER 8

Bare Earth and Stone Bones

Crow returned, as he had promised, and soon, he and Hoax were visiting often, as they used to. Crow would play his fiddle and Lumina would dance. The sylphs would spin leaves for the silver cat to bat at as Hoax jested and told stories to make them laugh. Sometimes Ember would come to light their nights and dance. And for a while it was as if everything was as it had been, mostly.

There was the White Stag, and his occasional visits to the glade. Which Lumina found unsettling, but not necessarily unpleasant. He would speak with Meg, asking after her and her charge; and inquire about the boy and how he fared. But he never once asked about the boy's blood, so the blood thorn remained safely in Lumina's bag, where it had been since she had taken it from the rose.

The Fairy Queen brought the boy every fortnight, as promised. There was no more mention of her helping Lumina. She was seemingly content to while away the day in Lumina's glade or down by the lake. Nor did she really speak of the Goblin King or his kingdom. Although there was always a soft concern in her eyes whenever she spoke with Lumina, which was more than a little unnerving.

But there was one thing that had Lumina looking forward to the queen's visits; she was often able to feed the boy. She believed the fruits and nuts, and a bit of goat's milk, did some good. At least his hands seemed less gaunt when she held them, and the hollows were gone from his cheeks when she touched them. When he would eat, his eyes would clear, and for a while he would seem to see the world around him as it was, though she could not say whether that was a good thing.

Lumina came to realize that the tear shed by him that first day was not because of a horror that he had endured, but a joy that he had lost. She also decided that at least in this, the Fairy Queen was not hurting the boy on purpose, but rather that the faerie realm was not for mortal minds.

But it would all wash away as soon as the queen took his hand in hers, and a mad kind of joy would fill him once again. And though Lumina could not truly understand, it made her very sad.

There were some welcome changes as well. Meg and the nanny goat for one, especially as far as the silver cat was concerned. The gruagach would freely share out the goat's milk if the boy was not due to visit.

The other was the frequent visits that Lumina made to the house at wood's edge and the growing friendship with the eld woman that lived there.

So it was that summer made its way towards autumn.

One crisp September morning found Lumina sitting atop the eld woman's table, on her sachet of dried rose petals and marjoram, sipping tea from her blue thimble.

Across from her sat the eld woman herself, porcelain tea cup in hand, light glinting off its golden edges.

They had thrown open all the doors and windows, letting the brisk breeze swirl in to where they sat. The garden beyond was just beginning to don its autumn dress, with an edge of crimson here and a kiss of gold there. But that was not what Lumina saw as she looked out through the window next to where she sat. Her thoughts were much further away, out across the highlands now most likely purple with blooming heather, to a dark lake edged by sharp hills where ruined towers quietly crumbled.

"You seem distracted today," the eld woman observed.

"Perhaps I am, just a little," she admitted, turning her attention back to her companion. "Tell me, have you ever met the Goblin King?"

"Many times," the eld woman answered, stirring more honey into her tea. "Why do you ask?"

"Did you know I am to marry him?" Lumina asked.

The eld woman stopped stirring her tea.

"I did not," she admitted. "How did that come about? If you don't mind me asking."

"I owed him a debt, and this Midsummer's Eve, he called it due."

"What debt could you have possibly owed that he would name such a price?" the eld woman asked, setting the little spoon down and taking a sip of her tea.

"When I first found the silver cat as a kitten I did not know how to feed him," Lumina said. "So I went to a farmhouse and took the tribute left there for the goblins."

"A bold choice," said the eld woman.

"No choice at all," Lumina replied. "The kitten would have died if I had not and I have no regrets." She looked over fondly to where the silver cat was napping in a sunbeam. "However, I would certainly be more at ease with paying my debt if I did not feel like this was only a game between him and the Fairy Queen with me in the middle, nothing more than a leaf tossed about in a gale."

"That explains much," the eld woman said with a wry smile. " And I do understand how you feel because I too was once in a similar position, and it was not a comfortable place to be in. Still, it ended well for me."

"Did it? You owed the Goblin King a debt as well?" Lumina asked curiously.

The eld woman shook her head. "It is a long story, but one could say it was almost the other way 'round."

"Would you tell me?" Lumina asked holding out her blue thimble for the eld woman to refill.

"If you wish me to," the eld woman said, leaning forward to pour the tea.

"Have you ever wondered why Crow and Hoax call me 'eld woman'?" she asked. Lumina shook her head, having never truly given it a thought. The woman chuckled.

"I suppose I should not be surprised. Most fairies will give you every name, but their own," she said, leaning back and taking a sip from her own cup. "Eld woman is a name that comes from the elder tree, or Elder Tree Mother as she was called then, and was often given to the healing woman of my village. Which is what I was, though that was a long time ago. A very long time ago now, I guess."

"I had also been born with the sight, which meant I could see what other mortals could not. So, I often saw the fae as I roamed the woods in search of the plants that I needed to work my trade. However, I never let on that I could see them, so they let me be, going about their business as I went about mine. Then one evening I stayed later in the wood than I was wont to do. Twilight was falling when I came across a white stag. There he stood as brilliant as a star, with a night-black raven perched in his silver antlers. I could not help but give myself away. What's more, I could see him for what he truly was.

"I offered him a bit of honeycomb, but then I heard the baying of the hounds. He made to leap away, but I stopped him, offering my help. With red thread I tied bells to his antlers and set a charm on them that would offer him a respite from those who hunted him, but would have no effect on any who would shelter him.

"But even good deeds have their price. As you well know," sighed the eld woman. "Shortly after that, my village began to suffer many hardships. For three years, droughts plagued us; crops would not grow; children sickened and died. And I was the only one who could see what was causing our sorrows. It was the fae who held back the clouds that would bring the rain. They put changelings in every cradle, and dug up all the seed that had been planted, so that it shriveled, unsprouted on the ground.

"I did not know then what had set the fair folk against us. I tried to placate them and when they would not be appeased, I tried to banish them."

"To banish them? Are you a priestess then?" Lumina asked. "Or a witch?"

"I have been called both, and many other names besides. I have knowledge of plants and the seasons. I can see the unseen, and I use power from all of them to do things others cannot. Call it what you will," answered the eld woman, sipping her tea.

"Do you use it to do harm?" Lumina asked, though she would find such a thing hard to believe.

"Who can say?" said the eld woman. "When you help one, sometimes another suffers. But no, my intentions were never to do harm. Yet the people of my village drove me out anyway. Though I had healed them when they were sick and blessed their unions. As midwife, I had even helped bring many of them into the world. And maybe that was why they only drove me away, instead of killing me outright. The fairies, on the other hand, had no soft memories to stay their hands. They tormented and chased me into the wood.

"And there was the white stag as though he was waiting for me. He bade me jump on his back, and away we went, the very bells I had given to him protecting us both as we fled. He brought me to this house and its garden, which were already here. They welcomed me as if they had been waiting for me all along.

"I was so grateful to him that I gave up the sight in one of my eyes," she said, her fingers coming to rest gently beneath the eye that looked as though it were filled with gray storm clouds, "in order to return his sight. However, I could not make them flesh again. Once he had his sight, he found his human shape, and the hunt could no longer pursue him."

She smiled fondly to herself. "Straight from my door he went, crossing the moorlands to the place where once stood his family's keep. Others gathered to him, and eventually they called him their king."

Lumina's brow furrowed. "How long ago was this?" she asked.

"Three centuries, this coming Hollentide Eve," said the eld woman.

"Three centuries?" Lumina exclaimed. "I did not know that mortals were so long lived."

"Most are not," the eld woman admitted, "but this garden holds many secrets and cares for those who care for it. I am happy here and do not regret the price I paid so that the white stag could regain his sight. He has proven himself true over the centuries and I have never found cause to doubt his word."

The morning was not much older when it found Lumina and the silver cat just outside the eld woman's garden gate.

"Tell me this dearest," she said as she peered through the trees to the moors beyond. "How am I to know the truth if I have not seen it?" she asked.

"Well Mistress, one would have to ask if you looked."

"Exactly my point dearest. I must go and look before I can see the truth," she said with a finality of one who has made up their mind to walk the gallows. "Can you take me to the Goblin King's Keep?"

"All the way this time?" he asked.

"Yes, dearest. All the way," she said. "Though doom may be my destination."

"It won't be," he replied as he headed off towards the purple moorlands.

The afternoon sun shone brightly down on them as they passed beneath the gateway of the ancient ruin. But this time, the silver cat did not head towards the battlements. Instead he pushed his way through the courtyard's tall grass to a doorway at the base of a large tower. Shafts of sunlight made golden pathways into the dim grotto, gilding the fern and rock roses that grew in the chinks and crannies along the walls. Everywhere else starry eyed moss covered the stones like an emerald dress.

The silver cat walked around the room's edge on silent feet. Lumina could not pull her eyes from the yawning hole in the center of the floor and the stygian darkness that filled it.

"Why are we here, dearest?" she asked the silver cat. "I thought the entrance was above?"

"Yes, one of them," he said, never stopping in his circuit. "The Mirror Gate, it's called. But it only opens once a day and you have to know when. Mine is a surer way. Do not worry Mistress, I use it all the time."

"Do you?" she said inquiringly. Her companion chose not to answer.

Thrice by thrice he circled the room, then without warning, leapt straight into the oubliette. A scream stuck in Lumina's throat as she held tight to the cat's silver fur;

however, it was not at the bottom of a dank hole that they landed, but rather at the edge of a bustling marketplace.

Dark gray pillars rose up smooth and straight all around them, like a forest of silver beech trees. Amidst the trunks a great many stalls and carts were set up, their wares out on display. There were even some shops, their fronts open wide to all the passers-by.

The silver cat strode out boldly into the goblin market. Everywhere Lumina looked, tables or mats were piled high; some with cloth, some with gems, some with fruit the likes of which no human garden had ever seen.

Others held more curious things... a woman's tears, a heart's wings, a child's dreams. They filled jars of alabaster and plates of gold. They overflowed from wooden bowls and cauldrons made of copper or stone.

Milling through it all was a host of creatures. Cloven-hoofed or talon-footed, with tufted ears or twitchy tails, she had not seen such a variety even amongst the Goblin King's entourage on Midsummer's Eve. Some were as small as Lumina herself, others towering so high their heads were lost in the gloom above, if indeed they had heads at all.

They passed by hearthfires where salamanders danced happily, writhing about in strangely colored flames of violet, green or the brightest blue. Sylphs rushed by them, running their fingers through the cat's fur, as they raced through the booths like children playing tag.

The silver cat made his way through all of it with the surety of one who had been there many times, his tail held proudly in the air as he walked between the stalls, like a knight's pennant proclaiming to all and sundry of his arrival.

"A fine catch, master cat!" a bogle called out from where he stood next to a shabby cart. His whiskers twitched in his rat-like snout as he watched them approach.

"I can give you fair trade for her," he promised in a smooth voice, as sticky as a spider's web. "Milk from Bo-finn perhaps, or salmon from the Well of Segais?"

A low growl rumbled in the silver cat's throat. "Have a care what you say, little rat or I'll pick my teeth with your bones."

"Peace! Peace, master cat!" the bogle said, and there was no wheedling in his tone now. "I meant no disrespect."

The silver cat continued on without a word, his tail twitching, his gait stiff legged with annoyance. Lumina assumed that the bogle had been asking after her. It was a strange thing indeed to have someone offer to buy her, and from the silver cat no less. She did not think she cared for it at all.

They wound their way through the market. Some paid them no mind while others nodded at the silver cat or hailed him as they passed by. He, in turn, ignored them, in his usual cat-like way.

They had gone down several more rows in much the same manner, when one of the merchants actually came out from behind his stall to greet them, his shell-crusted coat clacking and clattering as he did so.

"Well-a-day my friend," the shellycoat said to the silver cat. "What a lovely sprite you have there. Is she for sale?"

"No, good shellycoat, she is not. She is in fact my mistress," replied the silver cat with evident pride.

"Your mistress! I beg your pardon," the shellycoat apologized, doffing his weedy cap. "But I have to ask, Master cat; does our King know one of the Queen's is in his realm?"

"If he doesn't, he will soon enough," replied the silver cat, flicking his tail dismissively. "Besides which, my mistress is the Lady of the Glade and is no one's but her own." With that the silver cat turned to leave, heading back out into the river of market goers.

"Indeed. Well, no offense intended," the shellycoat called after them, "and if there is time on your return trip Master cat, stop by. I have a fish you may like, delicate and white, from the deepest depths of the sea."

After they had moved further down the row Lumina asked curiously, "Tell me, dearest, why is it okay for one merchant to ask my price but not another?"

"That's easy Mistress," said the silver cat. "You can't trust the bogle. He would be as happy to sell *me* as he would be to sell *to* me. The *shellycoat*, on the other hand, does good business. He often gives me fish."

"And what do you give him?" Lumina asked.

"Give him?" said the cat a little puzzled. "No, Mistress, he gives me the fish."

"So, it is a gift then?" Lumina asked a little worriedly. "Be careful of taking such gifts, dearest. Rarely does one of us, goblin or fae, give a gift freely."

"Ah, but you saved me freely," the silver cat pointed out.

"So I did dearest, and I am the happier for it," the sprite said, smiling tenderly.

"And I am sure the shellycoat is happier for giving me fish as well," her companion said assuredly.

The market seemed endless but eventually Lumina was able to catch glimpses of the Keep's crimson banners. They turned a corner to find a pair of enormous green paws blocking their path. They were attached to a gigantic dog who regarded them with burning red eyes.

"What do you have there, friend cat?" he asked, leaning his great shaggy head down as if to get a closer look. "She is lovely. I would be happy to buy her from you."

His words were amiable, as friendly as the shellycoat's, Lumina thought. But the silver cat, horn-eared and bristling, obviously did not agree.

"She is not for sale," the silver cat said with some caution and a great deal of cat hauteur.

"Are you sure?" the goblin dog pressed.

"She is my mistress, cu sith. And so I am very sure that she is not for sale," he insisted cooly, the angry flick of his tail saying volumes more.

"Your mistress, huh?" said the cu sith, raising back up to his full and impressive height. "Quite the lovely sprite indeed. Though I wonder if our King would agree. Should I ask him?"

"Indeed you should," replied a jovial voice. "But when you do, I would suggest you watch your tongue, for it might be the last time you see it. The King sets great store by his intended bride."

The cu sith turned to look in the direction from which the voice had come. Lumina's gaze followed his to a vague figure leaning against one of the stone pillars, obscured by shadows, save for his smile which shone brightly from out of the gloom.

"His bride!" exclaimed the huge goblin dog. "Truly? Well who am I to stand in the way of a man's doom. My apologies," he said, bowing his shaggy head to Lumina as he took his leave of them.

As he walked off, the figure emerged from out of the shadows. Pale green eyes, bright and luminous, peered out at her with good humor from behind coal black bangs. Set high on the goblin's head was a pair of furry ears; small, pointed and as black as the waves of his hair they protruded from. Lumina watched them as they twitched in her direction. For a moment, she was overwhelmed with a sense of recognition.

"I know you," she said uncertainly.

"Do you?" he asked. The intentness of his gaze was incongruous with his wide, affable smile.

Lumina paused, unsure. It was as if a different answer sat on the tip of her tongue and she struggled to understand what it was.

"Of course," she said finally. "You danced with me in the round this past Midsummer's Eve. And brought me to the Goblin King when he asked his boon."

The goblin man chuckled, his gaze softening as its intensity drained away like water.

"So I did then, and so I am doing now," he said with a sweeping bow. "If you will follow me, my fair one."

Lumina nodded and he turned, heading off towards the Keep, the silver cat falling in step with him. Ahead, the market goers cleared a wide path for them.

"What should I call you?" Lumina asked, disturbed by the feeling that she should already know the answer.

"Your servant, fairest. Call me such if you will; for that is what I am," he said, his eyes shining down at her with good humor once again.

Two more turnings, and suddenly the stalls came to an abrupt end. The Keep's dark walls rose up ahead of them, crimson banners flowing down its sides, just as Lumina remembered. At its foot lay a wide river of clouds, shining softly in the never-ending twilight, as though the moon lay hiding beneath them.

A bridge of spun silver spanned its banks, a glittering pathway to the brooding keep on its far shore. They crossed over it, passing through the looming gateway at its end, and out into a courtyard beyond where she found the night sky stretched out at their feet. Silvered clouds raced just beneath them as far below, a crescent moon sailed gracefully along, a high-prowed ship on a starry sea.

In the center of this surreal nightscape stood the Goblin King, a vibrant star in a coat of garnet and gold. How he could be standing where he was, Lumina could not say. It looked to her as though there was nothing beneath his feet save open sky.

Open sky, which the silver cat did not hesitate to step out onto, striding up to where the King stood, as bold as brass.

"You came," said the Goblin King, reaching down to offer his hand to Lumina. As soon as she rested hers on his fingertip, she found herself standing taller, as it had been when he had last taken her to the Well of Stars.

The silver cat, undaunted by her sudden change in stature, leapt deftly to her shoulder. He leaned his silken cheek against hers and purred.

The Goblin King did not loose her hand as he led her towards the great doors, standing open at the other end of the courtyard. She, in turn barely noticed, busy marveling at the improbable night sky beneath her feet and the strangeness of walking on something where there should be nothing. It was stranger still to see the dark walls of the Keep rising up from this nothingness. She noticed then that the walls and towers surrounding her were a mirror to the ruins she had entered through, now made whole and lovely.

Through the great stone doors they went, down oddly lit corridors that twisted back onto themselves like serpents. At their end was a vast hall, warm and beckoning in contrast, with floors made of jasper and a ceiling of chalcedony. Between this earth and the sky stood great pillars of agate, topped with branches of beaten gold; an aurulent autumn wood crowned by an ethereal blue heaven.

Brilliant tapestries lined the walls and between them opened numerous doorways. From one such doorway, the most delicious smells emanated. As they passed, the silver cat leapt down from Lumina's shoulder and sauntered toward said doorway, tail held high.

Lumina stopped. "Dearest?" she called after him as he disappeared down the passageway.

"No need to worry, Mistress," his voice echoed back to her. "We are among friends after all and this is where they keep the cream."

The dark-haired goblin, who had been only a few steps behind them, stopped as well.

"I believe I will follow him," he said, giving her a saucy smile. "Friends or no, if I leave him to his own devices there will be no cream left in the crock by the time he is done. So, by your leave..." he said, bowing to her and giving her a wink. Then, not waiting to see if they said yea or nay, he headed off in the same direction as the silver cat.

"Those two are one and the same," said the Goblin King beside her. "With servants such as them, who needs kings?"

Lumina started to follow, but a gentle squeeze of her hand made her hesitate. She looked up to find him smiling softly down at her.

"Bide awhile with me, if you would," he said. "There is more I would like to show you, and the silver cat will still be here when we are done. There is more cream than he could ever finish, despite my knight's dire predictions."

She glanced once more down the passageway before nodding her acquiescence. They left the doorway behind, strolling out among the lofty pillars, alone in the vast hall. He led her past the obsidian throne, to a small bronze door behind it, nearly hidden beneath a large crimson banner.

It opened on silent hinges. Together they slipped through, entering into a round room filled with soft moonlight. Lumina could not see the ceiling above, but at her feet an extraordinary inverted tower plunged deep into the earth. Its walls were lined with slender columns behind which a sweeping staircase spiraled down to a bright silver disk of a floor, shining up from below.

"Just a little further," said the Goblin King, as he started down the steps, the moonlight through the arches beside them casting a carpet of silver-traced lacework at their feet.

Their journey was a silent one, the Goblin King offering no hint of their destination, and Lumina not asking. When they reached the bottom, she let go of his hand, stepping away from his side, and out into the shaft of light spilling down from above. It washed over her face as she looked up, back the way they had come. From below, the delicate colonnade now resembled the chambered whorls of a giant sea shell.

"What do you think?" her companion asked from beside her, having followed her out into the light. It fell sharply on him, plating his features in silver and onyx, as he watched her with shuttered eyes.

She answered honestly. "It is lovely," she said, simply.

"I wonder if you will think the same of the next place we go," he mused, as he turned back to the shadows. The Goblin King spoke softly. So softly that it left her wondering if he had meant for her to hear it at all.

He was standing in front of a simple, unassuming door, nearly lost in the gloom. Removing a key from his coat pocket, he unlocked it, leaving it open behind him for her to follow if she chose. After a moment's hesitation she did so, stepping out into what might have once been a garden, but was now nothing more than bare earth and stone bones.

She found herself in a pool of golden light. Behind her was the old wooden door she had come through, flanked by two gigantic trees. The light in which she now stood came from a lantern hanging within their branches.

She marveled at the size of the trees and the fact that they seemed to be the only living things there, realizing her mistake when she reached out to touch them. They too were stone, and had been for a very long time.

She turned back to the barren garden.

"What is this place?" she asked the Goblin King who was standing just a little ahead of her, at the edge of the golden light.

"A garden for you," he answered. "If you will have it."

"Mine?" Her brow furrowed with uncertainty.

"Yours," he said again.

Lumina stepped out from the lantern's light, into a softer, more silvery glow, which in its own way shone just as bright. A moon hung above her, full and heavy, though in the mortal world she was only a thin crescent in the night sky.

From her feet stretched a path of stark white stones, oddly luminous beneath the moon's pale light. It wound past columns and through archways that rose up out of the dark ground like old bleached bones. The dolorous landscape drew her, its twisting, morbid path enticing her to follow it. So she did, through hidden grottoes and past still pools with silent fountains that might have once whispered little secrets. And alongside tall walls, laced with archways. All through this silent, never-ending garden she wandered, the Goblin King following only a few steps behind, on feet as quiet as an owl's wings. So quiet in fact, that she could almost believe herself alone.

"Can anything grow here?" she wondered aloud, though whether she was asking herself or the one who followed her, she could not say. Even so, he chose to answer.

"I believe it would, if you so wished it. No one else could bring life to this desolate place," he said, his voice a wistful caress. "If you were to care for it, no doubt it would fill to overflowing."

Lumina found that she could not look at him while his longing still trembled across her skin. Her eye fell on a statue, the first she had seen in this place, almost hidden in the shadow of a broad arch. It was of a stag fashioned out of alabaster and silver.

She walked up to it, running her hand over its stone flank as she went, finding it cool and silken to the touch. Her fingers slid down its side, over the brawny shoulder, until she stood at its head. It was magnificent, powerful and unbowed. It stood as steadfast as a granite mountain, but its eyes held all the sadness in the world. She reached up to run her hand along its jaw.

"He is beautiful," she said, "but I feel like my heart is going to break from the look in his eyes." It was as the words left her mouth that she realized who the statue was of and her cheeks burned hotly.

She turned her gaze to follow that of the alabaster stag's. It was looking out into a wide circle, ringed with arches. From each flowed a path of white stones, converging in the center where another statue stood, its back to them.

Lumina walked out into the circle, following the path until she stood just behind the statue. It was of a woman, her arms held out in delightful abandon as she danced. Her hair, the deep blue of the evening sky, was carved from a single piece of lapis lazuli. Lumina circled the dancer until she could see her face... her own face, with eyes close and head tilted skyward, as if she smiled up into the shining light of the moon.

Lumina fell back a step, her back coming up flush against the Goblin King who stood behind her. He did not raise his hands to touch her, but neither did he move away.

"What is this?" Lumina asked, confused and perhaps a little frightened.

"Nothing for you to be afraid of," the Goblin King said softly into her ear. "This place is yours, and yours alone, to tend or neglect as you will."

He pressed a metal object into her palm. It was cold, so cold it burned. But she did not drop it, instead holding it tighter. Looking down she saw a key resting in her hand. The same key that the Goblin King had used to open the door that had led them to this neglected garden.

"Yours is the only key, to do with as you will. In fact you need do nothing at all if that is what you want.

But I hope that you will come here, plant your trees and flowers, and make a haven of it."

She turned to look at him and his eyes were no longer shuttered. She could see hope there, tempered by uncertainty and an old sadness. She smiled up at him, sure in the decision that she was about to make.

"I have something for you," she said, reaching into the spider-silk bag at her hip. She pulled from it the blood thorn that she had been carrying for so long. A look of puzzlement crossed his face as she held the thorn out to him.

"You made a request of me some time ago so that you could be certain that the child was indeed your kin," she explained. "This thorn holds that boy's blood."

Taking the thorn from her, he regarded it for a moment, then quickly pierced the palm of his heart hand. A bright drop of blood welled up, like a garnet nestled on the white silk of his skin. A single drop formed on the tip of the thorn which he still held above his palm. It slowly fell to mingle with the blood that lay there.

A faint chime rang through the air as like called to like, the blood singing its recognition of its own.

"So, he is kin to you," said Lumina, hopeful that some good might come from that fact.

The Goblin King nodded his head. "The boy is indeed the seed of my brother's line," he acknowledged.

"Then you are obligated to do what you can for him?" she asked.

"I am," he agreed. "And I fear that means that I must hold you to your debt."

"I did not give you the blood thorn in the hope that I would be released from what I owe you," she said earnestly, for that had never been her motivation. "I gave it to you, Lorne, because you said it would be easier to help him if he were truly of your blood."

"Lorne?" he said, his eyes shuttered once more. "So, she gave you my name."

Lumina stilled, just realizing what it was she had said. "I..." she began, but the Goblin King pressed his finger to her lips, silencing her apology.

"There is no need," he said. "I would have given it to you eventually. You are a safer keeper of it than the one who gave it to you. And I certainly have no objections to hearing my name on your lips." A smile passed over his own, for a brief moment. "But still, it was not hers to give." There was anger in the set of his jaw as he turned away.

He left through a different arch than the one through which they had entered. And so, Lumina learned that she need never fear getting lost. For it seemed that all paths led back to the door from whence they had come, just as they all met in the circle's center.

It was not long before they stood in front of the old wooden door; with its pool of golden light and its stone trees standing sentinel on either side. The Goblin King passed through it, disappearing into the shadows beyond, but Lumina did not follow him immediately. Instead she stopped, reaching into one of her coat's many pockets where there was always something of one sort or another. Mostly seeds and baubles like the one she had given to Crow so long ago. She pulled out two fat seeds that shone like teardrop shaped pearls in her hand. One was from her own wild rose, the other from the sweet briar at the Well of Stars.

At the foot of each of the sentinels, she planted first one seed, then the other. As she did, she spoke to it of life, of the silver light that would nurture it and the dark soil that would protect it. No sooner had the words passed her lips, than the tiniest of tendrils, delicate and determined, began pushing their way up through the earth.

Light hearted, she followed the Goblin King back through the garden door.

CHAPTER 9

The Witch's Garden

The Fairy Queen sat on the branch of a hazel tree, her ringlets bouncing merrily as she swung her legs back and forth. The motion set the springy bough swaying and dipping beneath her like a fractious horse.

Lumina sat next to her on the branch while the boy lay sprawled on a bed of clover, his lips stained with blackberry juice. The sun smiled down on him, stroking his burnished gold hair and kissing his eyelids, now closed over eyes of the bluest-green.

Even as Lumina watched the sleeping boy, her mind was wandering elsewhere. Mostly she missed Crow and Hoax, whom she had not seen for several days. Though more than once she found her thoughts turning to the barren gardens and the goblin who had gifted them to her.

The Fairy Queen gave her legs a particularly powerful swing, so that the branch shied violently beneath her, before settling down once again.

"Has Lorne come to see you again?" the Fairy Queen asked, in her sweet child's voice.

"He has, a few times," Lumina answered, saying nothing of her own visit to the goblin's city.

"More than a few times, I'm sure," The Fairy Queen exclaimed, her eyes dancing merrily, as though they shared a secret. "And does he mention the boy?"

"He does," she said. "He often asks how he is faring."

"Does he?" said the queen, her face turning thoughtful and maybe a little sad. "That's good. But I should warn you that his interest in the boy does not necessarily mean that he holds only good will towards him. And the reason for that can be laid at my feet." The queen's large doe-soft eyes filled with regret as she smiled a sad little smile. "Lorne and his brother were once knights of my court. My beloved sun and moon. So beautiful, so full of the fire that mortal hearts hold. I loved them so! And for a while we were happy. But eventually his brother became discontent, wanting more. I would not let him be king to my queen, so he tricked a mortal girl into freeing him and stealing him away."

Crystalline tears filled the Fairy Queen's eyes, spilling down over her cheeks, splashing on to her little hands, and onto the comforting hand that Lumina had unconsciously laid on the queen's little finger. Any doubts that she may have had about the queen's sincerity were washed away with their passing.

"I was so hurt by Tam Lin's betrayal that I did something then that I wish had not. Since his brother was out of reach, I turned to Lorne and took my pain out on him. When I came to my right mind, I realized what I had done. I sent others of my court out to find him, to bring him back so that I could undo what I had done, but he was gone. For a hundred years they hunted after him to no avail. And now it is far too late, for as you can imagine, he is filled with bitterness and no longer trusts me."

Lumina nodded her sympathy. Patting the queen's

finger reassuringly. It made sense that one would feel angry if someone betrayed your love.

"Then I saw this boy playing in my wood. He looked so much like Tam Lin, golden and beautiful, I had to bring him to my court. Of course, when Lorne asked for him I could not refuse; after all, being blood of his blood, he does have a certain claim. But I am afraid that it may not be out of kindness that he asked for the boy. He suffered much for the brother whose line this boy belongs to. There is a reason why I insisted that he take a bride from my court. It means that I can offer the boy some protection. Regrettably, that is why you are now in the difficult position that you are in. But I have not forgotten my promise to free you little sister, and the stone that you brought to me has given me some insight as to how."

Lumina looked up into the queen's fathomless eyes and nodded. It would be wonderful for things to be as they had been; Crow playing his fiddle as she danced the world round.

"There is a garden at the edge of the goblin's wood. In this garden is an old, old apple tree. So old, its roots reach down through time itself. It would help if you bring me an apple from that tree. Any apple would do, but the last one of the season would be best. Be careful though," she warned. "A witch tends that garden and she is no friend to our kind. If she catches you, she might bind you or ask you for a promise of service in return for the apple."

Lumina found herself nodding in agreement, even though she knew the eld woman was her friend.

"Next, I will need water from a well that sits in the heart of the goblin's wood. But I cannot tell you how to draw it, nor what vessel will hold it."

Lumina continued to nod. In fact, she could not seem to stop nodding. She began to wonder if she would continue to nod until her head fell from her shoulders.

A flicker of movement drew her eye. The slightest breath from the boy, and she was back to herself. She stopped nodding, turning her eyes away from the Fairy Queen's gaze to look at him. His face was still round with youth, innocent and unguarded. He whimpered slightly and Lumina unconsciously started crooning to him as she had once done to the silver cat when he was young.

When she looked back at the Fairy Queen she found her little girl face as beautiful as the boy's, but with none of his innocence.

Still smiling, the Fairy Queen swung down from the branch with a grace no mortal child could ever possess.

"Then we shall see you again in a fortnight, little sister," she said. Waking the boy, she took him by the hand and led him off, back to fairyland.

The day had not started out stormy. It had actually been quite pleasant when Lumina and the silver cat first set out to visit the eld woman. But half way through the Goblin Wood, the winds picked up. When dawn came and the sun lifted her shining head, she did so behind a thick veil of clouds.

Now, as they approached the eld woman's gate, it was as black as night though sunset was still hours away. The rain had begun falling some time before, blown hard by sharp gusts of wind. As they passed beneath the old gate trees, Lumina felt a pull, steady and insistent. She slipped off the silver cat's back.

"Go on ahead dearest," she called back over her shoulder as she headed off deeper into the garden. "I will be in soon."

Lumina heard the silver cat behind her, yowling at the eld woman's door. She heard the door open, the eld woman's exclamation chasing after her as she walked down the garden's familiar paths.

"Ah, you silly thing! Does your mistress know that you're out in this weather..."

But it all seemed so far away. The need to see this apple, the one the Fairy Queen had spoken of, drew her on. The storm raged about her; a wild tempest whose song would have normally swept her up in its dance, yet this time she took no notice of it.

The tree she sought stood in the very middle of the garden. She walked up along the trunk, twisted with age, listening to the tree's slow, sleepy murmurings as she went. His roots were deep, his branches wide, and he was old, so very old. A gnarled, ancient apple tree that might have been planted at the very beginning of the world.

She found what she was looking for easily enough, and it was indeed the last apple. Small, round and red, it was perfect in every way. The picture of what all apples should look like, without a hole or blemish to mar its smooth skin.

Lumina's hand reached out of its own accord, an impulse filling her, cloaked in the guise of curiosity. Why this apple, she wondered. She had come to see it with no intention of plucking it, and yet, both her hands were reaching up to do just that.

"Lumina!" she heard the eld woman call her name. The urgency in her voice pulled at her.

She looked down to where the woman stood just below. The wind whipped wisps of her graying hair from out of its usually neat braid; the shawl around her shoulders streamed out behind her like a pennant.

"Lumina," the eld woman said her name again, her words clear and strong, despite the howling of the storm. "Are you going to take the apple?"

Lumina felt a reluctance to speak with the eld woman. However, looking down at the her, she was startled to see how old the eld woman seemed. And not just because of the shroud of mortality that all mortals wore. With this realization, the strange malaise she had been feeling left her. Lumina climbed down to a lower branch, to better speak with the woman who had become her friend.

"I would not have taken it without your leave," Lumina assured her, "but it drew me as soon as I arrived, like tides to the moon. And I found that I just had to see why the Fairy Queen would need such a thing."

"The Fairy Queen bade you bring it to her?" the eld woman asked.

"She did," Lumina replied.

"To what purpose?" wondered the eld woman. "Other than mischief, that is."

"She said it could help free me," Lumina admitted.

"And is that what you wish?" the eld woman asked. "To be free of your oath?"

"I... I don't know," Lumina confessed. "I truly don't. The Goblin King has been kind, but I would miss my glade and all those that live there." A great sorrow wrapped itself around her heart. "And what of Crow... and Hoax? Would I see them after I am wedded? Would I still be able to visit with you? I do not know."

"What I do know for certain is that I wish to help the boy whom the queen has carefully tucked away in her court. The boy who reminds me so much of the wet, broken kitten that I once found dying under a rose bush."

The eld woman sighed, and the wind seemed to sigh with her, settling down into soft swirling gusts.

"Then take the apple, Lumina, with my blessing. Take it and come in out of the wet." The eld woman turned and walked out into the gloom, towards the welcoming light of the cottage.

Lumina went back and plucked the apple from where it hung, wrapping her arms as far around it as she could. The old tree murmured sleepy questions as she ran lightly over the branches and down the twisted truck. She followed the path to the eld woman's door which opened as she approached.

The silver cat lay inside, curled up in front of the fire near an empty bowl. The eld woman was just sitting down, a cup of raspberry tea on the table in front of her.

Still holding the apple, Lumina leapt from dust mote to dust mote, first to the chair, then to the top of the table. She set the apple down on a small wooden plate that seemed to have been left there just for that purpose. The tiny blue thimble, brimming with tea, sat in front of her usual seat.

The eld woman did not smile and chat as she would have normally done, instead stared out at the storm through the window's heavy glass.

Lumina sat without speaking as well, understanding that there was more going on here than appeared on the surface, trusting that the eld woman would tell her when she was ready. Lumina sipped her tea and waited, watching the fire reflect off of the window's jewel-colored panes. The storm had picked up once again, grumbling and whistling through the cracks. Strangely enough though, the hedge bells were oddly quiet. Even with the winds shivering through its branches, only a soft chime rang out here and there.

Lumina had long since finished her tea before the eld woman broke her silence.

"Lumina, did the Fairy Queen tell you anything about the apple when she asked you to bring it to her?" asked the eld woman when she finally did speak. "Did she tell you what virtue it holds?"

"Not at all," Lumina replied, reaching out to stroke the apple. "She did say that its father tree was old and that his roots reached down through time itself. And I believe her. He was talking in his sleep as I walked along his branches. But nothing of the apple's virtue." Lumina looked up at the eld woman across from her and asked, "What virtue does it hold, other than the usual of its kind?"

"Immortality. Or infinity, depending on how it is used," the eld woman answered.

"Immortality? Why would she need such a thing? And how would such a thing be used to set me free? Perhaps... do you think it is for the boy?" Lumina speculated.

"I cannot say," the eld woman sighed. "Did she ask for anything else?"

"Water from a well at the heart of the goblin's wood. I believe she means the Well of Stars."

"Knowledge and destinies," said the eld woman, her forehead wrinkling with thought. "I don't know what game she plays, but I can tell you this; her heart is not the same as yours, my dear sprite. Do not judge her on what you, yourself have done. Had she found a kitten dying under a rose bush, she may have left it or she may have saved it. Then when it scratched her, she may have snapped its neck, only to cry brokenheartedly seconds later over its loss. She surely would not have seen the same kitten in a broken boy and set herself to save him. She is as a child. A beautiful, spoiled child, ruled by her whims with no true conscience. She may love you, hate you, and forget you all in a day."

"I do not doubt you," said Lumina. "She admitted what she had done to the Goblin King when he was still a knight of her court. Her regret at doing so seemed sincere. She told me that she had sent the hunt out to bid him return so that she could undo it and possibly make amends."

"Oh, I have no doubts she regrets what she did! After all, it is fae nature to say the truth. But the truth becomes a twisty thing when it comes to emotions and careful words can say one thing while meaning another," the eld woman warned. "But I will speak plainly; the Fairy Queen has no love for me. She has always hated that it was me, not she, who gave the white stag back his sight. And, she holds a grudge for my warding of him against the hunt. It was why she brought such grief to my village and in turn why I was driven out."

Lumina sighed deeply, feeling more than ever that she was caught up in events beyond her control.

"It may be our nature to speak the truth, but I will admit I cannot see the truth in all this. I am a grain of sand caught between the wind and the waves. The king and queen move me like a pawn in their game, and I have to wonder, was my debt really so large for the king to have asked me such a price in repayment? And I only seem to be acquiring more, because now I owe you a debt."

"No my dear, you could never have paid the debt owed me for this, so I give it to you freely, as a gift," said the eld woman, and again Lumina noticed time weighing heavy on her friend. "In the morning I will help you home with it."

From that point on, they spoke only of easy things and Lumina took note of the eld woman and how she differed from the picture painted by the Fairy Queen's words.

In the morning they left the witch's garden, the apple tucked safely in a pouch hung from the eld woman's wrist. They ambled amicably through the wood. The late summer sunshine sent streamers of light down through the heavy branches to glowing pools on the forest floor. The bells on the eld woman's walking stick chimed softly in natural accompaniment to the trees' ever-present whispers.

They stopped for lunch, and by evening, stood at the border stream. The silver cat took the pouch from the eld woman. Brushing once against her shins in farewell, he leapt lightly from stone to stone across the ford to the other side of the stream.

"It is a lovely place," the eld woman said, waving to Meg and the old nanny goat who was out grazing in the meadow.

"Would you like to come visit?" Lumina asked, excited at the thought of showing the eld woman all the places she had spoken of so often.

"Yes," the eld woman said wistfully, "but it is unwise for me to do so. The one who holds power on your side of the border stream has no love for me, and she would take great delight in having me so vulnerable. The goblin's wood offers me some protection beyond my own, and I am safe there. Maybe one day, there will be no need to worry about such things."

Lumina looked up at the darkening sky, disappointment sluicing through her. "Will you be safe traveling at night?" she asked. "Perhaps the silver cat should go with you?"

The eld woman laughed. "No, I will be fine. Nothing there will hurt me and I know the way very well. Take care and come see me soon."

With that, the eld woman turned and left, the welcoming shadows of the wood quickly wrapping her in their embrace.

When the eld woman left Lumina, she slowly made her way back through the dark wood. She felt tired, so very tired. It had been long, long years since she had last felt this way.

It was still early in her journey home when she saw a whisper of silver flash by out of the corner of her eye. She smiled to herself. It was as she had expected.

She walked around the bole of a gigantic oak, and there he was, just as she had first seen him those many years ago, glowing silver-white like a newly risen moon, an obsidian raven perched in the span of his magnificent antlers.

She stopped and scowled at them, her disapproval thick in the air. "I don't know what game you and the queen are playing, Lorne, but Lumina should not be a part of it," she said sternly. "She is a kind and guileless creature, with a caring heart. She is too small a thing to be caught in the middle of you two."

"Peace Arianna," the White Stag replied, cutting off anything further that she might have said. He moved towards her, changing into his more human seeming from one step to the next.

The eld woman had fallen into a stunned silence that was not brought on by his changing shape.

"Arianna," she said thoughtfully. "That was once my name. I had forgotten."

"But I have not," said the Goblin King, offering her his arm. "Will you walk with me?"

The eld woman accepted, linking her arm in his. They set out once more through the dark wood, walking easily together as they had many times before.

"Lumina is not as small a thing as you believe. Besides, it is not my game we play, but Maeve's. And I do not know all the rules yet. Nor do I yet understand her true goal," he admitted. "I swear to you, had I anticipated what she had in mind at midsummer, I would have made sure to have a plan in place. I did not bring Lumina into this willingly."

"Then take her out of it!" the eld woman insisted. "Release her from the debt she owes you. Find another way to save the boy."

"Just as I have told him," said the raven, leaning forward to address her from the Goblin King's other shoulder.

"It is far too late for that," said the Goblin King, answering the woman and ignoring the raven. "She has been seen now and Maeve's interest has been peaked. There is no turning back for either of us."

Then suddenly they were in front of the eld woman's garden gates, a journey that had previously taken most of the day made in less than a quarter of an hour. She chuckled.

"Something tells me you do not wish to speak of this," she said, looking up at her companion. He was smiling back at her warmly. Leaning down, he kissed her on her cheek.

"I promise you this, if I cannot woo her by our wedding day, I will release her from her debt and find another way to save the boy."

CHAPTER 10

Autumn Equinox

Lumina lay on a branch high up in Old Father Pine. She watched as an armada of cloud ships sailed across the deep blue sky. A cool wind tangled her hair as it whispered through the needles around her.

Only one other kept her company, though she could not see him. The music of his fiddle drifted down from the branches above, letting her know he was there.

Her thoughts were awhirl, as they often were now. The eld woman's gift of the apple unsettled her, as did many of the things that had been happening of late. Even the music of Crow's fiddle did little to take her mind off it all. A soft sigh escaped her lips, only to be carried swiftly away by the wind's cold kiss.

The music stopped. Turning her head up to see why, she found Crow perched just above her.

"Such a sigh, my Lady of the Glade," he said, his voice filled with soft concern. "If I didn't know better, I would say you are brooding."

"Brooding?" she asked, her gaze turning back skyward.

"Yes, brooding. Dwelling on thoughts that trouble you."

"Is that what it is called?" she said. "Then I suppose I am."

"I wonder... is it the Goblin King or the Fairy Queen that troubles your thoughts so?" asked Crow.

Although the geas, for geas she was sure it had been, not to speak of the Fairy Queen was gone, she still felt a great reluctance to speak of the Goblin King to Crow. In fact, she had not spoken to him of her troubles at all, yet she was unsurprised that he knew of them.

"Or is it the gift the eld woman gave you? I think it was a greater gift than you know," he said. "Did she tell you what virtue the apples from that tree hold?"

His tone, though light, caught her attention and added to the growing concern in her belly.

"She told me they hold the virtue of infinity or immortality depending on how it is used," she said, now quite certain she was about to learn something more of what that might mean.

"Yes, exactly," he said, his eyes sharp and penetrating. "Every year, old man apple bears twelve fruit. The eld woman eats one each month, for eleven months out of twelve, and for that month time passes her by. This means that she only ages for a single month for every year that passes. However, if the twelfth apple is taken from his branches, it will be seven years before the tree can bear fruit again."

Lumina's heart sank with grief as she began to understand the cost of the gift that the eld woman had given to her so freely.

"Is seven years a long time?" she asked.

"For a mortal, it can be" said Crow. "And since you are not mortal I must ask, why would you need such a gift?"

"The Fairy Queen asked me to bring her an apple from the old tree that grows in the witch's garden at the edge of the wood," she replied, her voice catching in her throat at the thought of the harm that she had caused her friend, inadvertent though it may have been.

"Did the Fairy Queen ask you for anything else?" he queried.

"Water from the well in the heart of the goblin's wood," Lumina answered.

"And what does she offer you in return for these things?"

"She believes she can find a way to free me from my debt," Lumina admitted.

"And is that what you wish, Lumina?" Crow asked softly, almost sadly.

Lumina sat up, drawing her knees to her chin. "I wish that I wasn't such a small thing, to be moved about in this game between the two courts. Though I suppose what I truly wish most of all is for things to stay as they are."

"Ah, my Lady, you are not as small thing as you believe yourself to be," Crow assured her, leaping lightly down to the branch on which she sat. He squatted there with his arms on his knees, perching just in front of her feet. "And I wish that I could grant your second wish, but nothing stays the same forever." He reached out to stroke a taloned finger softly against her cheek. Then taking both her hands in his, he stood up, bringing her with him.

"Now let this go," he said, "at least for tonight. Call your salamander and call your sylphs. We can pass this night dancing in the firelight as the summer passes into the fall. And for a little while, there need be nothing more than that."

Heeding Crow's advice, she let go for that moment what she could not yet change. Hand in hand, they headed down to the lakeshore, telling the sylphs their plan as they went. The sylphs raced on ahead, singing and laughing, the tall dry grasses rattling with their passage.

When Lumina and Crow reached the edge of the lake, they found the sylphs had already been busy. Gale had spun a circle flat, leaving only bare earth in his wake. Zephyr and Mistral, in turn, had gathered all the dry grasses, twisting them together into a tall straw man at the center.

At Serene's direction, a line of little frogs hopped from the lake carrying pale, smooth stones in their mouths. They laid them in a circle around the straw man, while Meg and Hoax brought bundles of dead wood to lay at his feet. Soon the pile towered high above their heads.

As the light in the sky faded, Lumina took the tiny box of ashes from her spider-silk bag, sprinkling a little over the waiting wood. In a short while, Ember was dancing on the pyre, the sylphs whirling swiftly around him, stroking him over and over again, until he stood taller than a man, his fire reaching up high into the heavens.

Crow's fiddle poured out a wild tune that set the world awhirl. The moon was smiling down on them and the air was as heady as wine as they danced. Their shadows, now giants, leapt high in the fire's light.

They danced and laughed as they sang the moon down. Now, in the darkest hours just before dawn, almost all had succumbed to sleep. Lumina lay curled up asleep with the silver cat at the edge of the fire's light. The winds had gone long ago, and the great bonfire was now only a pile of embers. The salamander sat amongst them, running his fingers through the glowing coals making them crackle and pop. Across from him sat Crow, legs folded up tailor fashion, his arms resting on his knees.

"You are not truthful with her," said the salamander, breaking the silence that had wrapped around them. His gaze was sharp as he looked straight at the goblin, instead of through him as he normally would have.

"Careful salamander, I will not have you trifling with this," the goblin warned, in a voice that assumed obedience.

"I have no fear of you, fairy lord. My loyalty is not yours to command," the salamander retorted. "If you will not tell her, I will."

"Why would you care, I wonder? This plane is not yours, only one you touch on occasion."

"Because just as he is your liege man," the salamander said, gesturing at Hoax, "so I am hers.

"Her liege man?" said Crow, flicking a small twig at the salamander who caught it, turning it to ash in a flash of flame. "I think I am not the only one who is not entirely truthful. Does she know how she bound you the first time she gifted you with a strand of her hair? Or did you ask for that gift, and bind yourself?"

"She does not know," the salamander admitted, leaving the second question unanswered.

"In all those years, you chose not to tell her?" Crow asked.

"No," he said, another glowing coal falling to ash under his fingers.

"And why is that?" Crow persisted.

"Because one such as she would want to set me free. It is a freedom I do not wish for," he said, his gaze turning to the figures sleeping just at the edge of the firelight. "I would much prefer not to lose her company."

"Then perhaps I do not tell her for the same reasons that you do not."

"Perhaps," Ember said, "but not entirely."

"No, my friend, not entirely," Crow agreed softly.

The whisperings of Old Father Pine drew Lumina from her sleep. She woke, still curled up with the silver cat at the edge of the dance circle. Her eyes opened on a pearly dawn sky overhead.

Hoax and Crow were gone, as were the sylphs and Ember. Meg lay not far away, blanketed beneath her long hair, the nanny goat grazing close by. It was a morning like any other, save for those whisperings of Old Father Pine.

Usually his voice was sleepy or soothing, but this morning it beckoned, inviting her to come see something wondrous. Slipping out from her soft bed, she followed the murmurings till they led her to a cluster of rocks on the far side of the pine tree.

There, growing in a small depression, sheltered on all sides by mossy rocks, was a tiny seedling. Its trunk was as slender as Lumina's finger, its top crowned by a tuft of bright green needles. She brushed her hand over them lightly.

"He is beautiful," she said to Old Father Pine. "I am sure I can find a good place for him to grow. In fact, I have a perfect place. A place where he can grow as tall as he wants."

Few of the great pine's offspring ever managed to take root in his shadow, so he was understandably proud. He also worried the seedling would not thrive if it was to stay where it was. So a short time later, the seedling sat at the edge of the glade, its roots bundled up in a small lily pad that Serene had given her. In front of it was the silver cat, sitting up tall, looking imperiously down at the spot where his mistress was standing, the little tree beside her.

"I am sorry Mistress, what are you asking me to do?"

"I am asking you to help me carry this little seedling to the Goblin King's Keep," Lumina said patiently, not for the first time.

"I still don't understand," said the silver cat.

"Dearest," she said, her exasperation plain. "You know perfectly well what I am asking of you."

"Yes," the silver cat admitted with bemused patience. "I understand that you want me to carry that seedling."

"You do?" Lumina said, bafflement replacing exasperation.

"Yes. But I am a cat," he explained.

"And why does that matter?" Lumina asked.

"Cats don't carry things," he said matter-of-factly. "That's what ponies and phookas are for."

"Neither are here, dearest. And you carry things," she pointed out. "After all, what do you do with the mice you catch?"

"I eat them."

Eventually, the silver cat acquiesced. They left the glade, the tiny tree safe in its lily pad satchel, hanging from his mouth by a handle made of twisted grass. Head held high because the needles kept tickling his nose, they crossed the stream, passing into the goblin's wood amid the silver cat's muffled grumbles.

The going was slow. It was just before midnight when they reached the eld woman's house. The windows were all dark.

"I don't wish to wake her, dearest. We can sleep in the bed of thyme that grows under the south window. The one nearest the spring."

That was where the cat took them, setting the seedling quickly down near the spring. He drank his fill of the cold water while Lumina gave a little to the seedling.

"Thank you, dearest," Lumina said, smoothing down his whiskers on one side before reaching up to scratch under his chin. A deep purr rumbled in his throat. The silver cat gently brushed his cheek affectionately along her shoulder.

"I am going off to hunt," he told his mistress before heading out into the night.

She wished him luck, then set off on her own errand, making her way down the now familiar garden to the old apple tree. Up the twisting pathways of his trunk she ran, just as she had ten days past. She found where she had plucked the last apple from its stem. Lightly stroking the branch from which it had hung, she began to dance, and then she began to sing.

She sang of life and vitality, of friendship and a gift freely given. With each note she gave a little of herself, her essence, her life force to the ancient apple tree. Fairy lights followed in her wake, green and gold and sapphire blue as the sap quickened under her feet. She sang and danced till she felt she had become a mere shadow of herself, a wraith on the wind.

"Enough, daughter," the old tree sighed. "Your gift is accepted. It will not take seven years, but only three till I bear fruit again. But, there will be only eleven for five years after that. One must still be left in my branches every year, as before. It is all I can offer."

"Thank you, old father," Lumina said tiredly.

She made her way back to the spring where the seedling sat, its needles happily waving in the breeze. The silver cat had not returned, so she curled herself up around the bundled roots of the seedling, where she promptly fell asleep.

Lumina woke up still curled around the seedling, and the silver cat curled up around her. The eld woman stood next to the spring, kettle in hand, still wearing her night rail, a thick shawl drawn tight across her shoulders.

"Good morning," she said, bending over to fill the kettle with water that was pouring out a stone spout. "There was no need for you to sleep out here."

Lumina sat up and brought the seedling closer to the spring so she could give him some water.

"The house was already dark when we arrived," she said, scooping water out of the spring with her hands and carefully pouring it onto the little tree so that it trickled down the trunk to the roots.

"Who do you have there?" the eld woman asked, setting her kettle to the side and kneeling down to get a closer look at Lumina's charge.

"A pine seedling that was growing in the glade, isn't he adorable!" Lumina said, beaming proudly at the tiny tree. "His father tree is the lone pine that shades my wild rose. We stay in a den beneath his roots in the winter. He told me of this seedling and asked if I could find a place for it to grow. His progeny rarely take root, and when they do, they are never able to grow in his shadow."

The eld woman brushed a fingertip over the tiny tree's needles. "He is a fine tree," she said. "He would be welcome in my garden if you do not already have a place in mind."

"That is very kind, but..." Lumina hesitated a little, a blush blooming across her cheeks, "the Goblin King gave me a garden and I thought I could plant him there," she said.

"A garden? Where?" the eld woman asked.

"In the Keep," Lumina answered.

"Truly? Why don't you come in and tell me about it

over tea," said the eld woman as she picked up her kettle and stood.

Lumina looked over at the seedling. "I really wanted to reach the Keep and possibly return before nightfall."

"Come in and have some tea, tell me about your garden, and afterward I will go with you to the Keep. It would be nothing for me to carry the seedling and I have to go to the market anyway."

The silver cat spoke up. "I think it's a good idea, Mistress," he said. "And if the eld woman carries the little tree it's much less likely that it will get eaten."

"Eaten?" Lumina said, her eyes narrowing.

"Most likely," said the silver cat matter-of-factly, "especially if it kept putting its needles up my nose."

The cold autumn winds blew into their faces as they set out across the moorlands. The sky was impossibly wide above them, that brilliant blue that only comes with the harvest. Lumina rode on the eld woman's shoulder close to her ear, so that she could be easily heard. The silver cat wandered hither and thither around them.

"I spoke with Crow," Lumina said, the wind tugging at her words. "He told me more about the gift you gave me, and the price you'll pay for giving it to me."

"Did he?"

"Yes, my friend, he did. Why did you give me such a precious gift?" she asked curiously.

A warm smile lit the eld woman's face. "I would like to say it was because you are my friend and I wish to help you. And that is true, but if I am to be honest, it is more for him than you. All the omens tell me that no matter how things may be perceived, this could lead to his happiness. And I would do much to help him find that."

"The him you speak of, you mean the Goblin King?" asked Lumina.

The eld woman nodded.

"I don't understand," Lumina continued. "You have already given up your sight for him. Why are you willing to give up your immortality? Do you love him so much?" she asked, her middle unexpectedly twisting about on itself like a nest of snakes.

The eld woman laughed. "I have never been immortal nor would I wish to be! Even if I was, giving up such a thing would not be the sacrifice that you think it would be. Immortality is a hardship for a mortal soul. Aging normally only one month for every year has allowed me to live for hundreds of years with a few hundred more to look forward to. That may not seem like such a long time to one such as you, but for the mortal mind, it is a very long time indeed."

"Besides," she said, her wide grin softening to a tender smile. "I do hold him in great affection. Our friendship has spanned centuries and he has always been kind to me. I can think of no one else, past or present, who is more deserving of happiness."

"Except perhaps, yourself," said Lumina. "You have a generous heart, and I told old man apple so. I danced along his branches and sang to him. Now it will be only three years, not seven, before he will bear fruit again.

Although, he said that for five years after that he will only bear eleven apples and one must still be left on his branches by year's end."

The eld woman chuckled. "The Fairy Queen will not thank you for giving those years back to me. Best not to tell her when next you two speak," she said.

"Best not to," Lumina agreed.

CHAPTER 11

Lumina Dreams
of Crows

It was mid-afternoon when they reached the ruined keep. They passed through the crumbling gate, but once through, the eld woman did not go up to the battlements and the Mirror Gate, as Crow had.

Nor did she lead them to the tower, and the oubliette beneath. Instead, she made her way through the bailey towards the keep proper. There amidst the berry brambles was a heavy oak door, bound in iron.

It stood alone, shaded by blackthorn trees. Its posts and lintel were made of stone. But if there had ever been walls to either side of it, they had long since fallen. A narrow path led them through the brambles to it. The latch holding it closed was made of iron. And though those of fae blood had little tolerance for iron, it was of no bother to the eld woman. She reached out and lifted the latch, pulling the door open. With Lumina on her shoulder and the silver cat at her heels, the eld woman stepped through the doorway into the goblin market.

It was a different part from where the silver cat had last brought Lumina. Here the carts were filled with fruits and roots. Vegetables were piled high in baskets, and flowers hung down around them in curtains. Small chests overflowed with seeds like gems in a king's counting room.

Lumina was enchanted. She leapt down from the eld woman's shoulder to a table so that she could walk among the chests. She ran her hands through the seeds, feeling them slide through her fingers as they told her stories of faraway lands. She lingered on a single pair of seeds nestled in a small soapstone box. They lay in their mossy bed, shimmering like two pearls in green velvet.

The eld woman had continued to the next stall over, where beautiful glass bottles held fragrant oils, and brightly glazed bowls were piled high with frankincense, copal and myrrh. The merchant greeted the eld woman warmly, paying no attention to Lumina as she ran her hands over the pair of seeds again. She listened as they told her of delicate pink blossoms and deep red fruit, heart-shaped and marvelously sweet.

"I understand that they are from a very old cherry tree," a man said from behind her. The sepulcher voice was deeply familiar, whispering over her skin like ghosts. Smiling, she turned and stumbled. The goblin standing there was not the one whom she had expected. Instead she found the Goblin King, dressed in a fine evergreen coat, his hair shimmering across his shoulders like moonbeams in a night dark forest.

He reached out to steady her as she stumbled. As soon as her hands touched his fingers, she was standing next to him, a great deal taller than she had been a moment before. The change in her stature had startled her, but it had also given her time to get past her confusion.

"Well met, my Lady," he said, smiling down at her, his hands still holding hers as gently as if they were holding butterflies. "Were you on your way to see me?"

Lumina's cheeks warmed. The Goblin King had honestly never crossed her mind when she had decided where she was going to plant the little tree.

"After a fashion," she hedged. "I was actually going to visit the garden. I brought something to plant there."

She turned to where the eld woman stood, holding out the seedling and smiling at them. Letting go of the Goblin King's hands, she reached out and took the little tree from the eld woman, marveling at how tiny it now looked in her hands. She turned back to the king.

"Isn't he perfect?" she said proudly, excitement quickly replacing the moment's awkwardness. She held the little tree up for him to see. "He is the progeny of the lone pine in my glade. Old Father Pine asked if I could find a place for him to grow, so I brought him here. I have a few other seeds as well..."

She looked up and her tongue froze. The anticipation and joy that filled the king's face sparked a warmth in her chest, calling forth an answering smile from her own lips.

Apparently she was not the only one affected by the king's mood. Silence filled the market around them as all present froze with shock. When the noise did resume, it had a different quality to it, and even the air seemed lighter.

The Goblin King's smile was radiant as he looked at her from behind the little tree's fuzzy needles which she was still holding between them. He brought his hands up to cup hers.

"He is a lovely tree," he said.

Flustered, Lumina looked away towards the eld woman who watched them with a soft expression and warm smile.

"The eld woman helped me carry him," she said.

"That was kindly done," he said, turning to follow her gaze. "Thank you."

Despite the hubbub of the market, soft gasps rippled out around them.

The eld woman tsked. "There is never a debt among friends," she said, a trace of admonishment coloring her tone.

The Goblin King bowed his head to her.

"Will you come with us to the Keep, eld woman?" he asked.

"No," the eld woman declined. "I still have business here and after that I think I will head home. It's best at this time of year if I don't stay away too long."

"As you wish," he said. "I will send someone to keep you company on your way."

"And I can guess who that someone will be," the eld woman said ruefully. "I am not sure if what you offer is a boon or a punishment. I *am* sure my ride home will not be a straight one."

"Mostly likely not," the dark-haired goblin said as he strolled up, laughter rolling his words out in front of him like marbles. "But you will come home... eventually." He winked at her.

"Do you wish me to stay with you?" Lumina asked, leery of the mischief dancing in the dark-haired goblin's eyes.

"There is no need, dear" said the eld woman coming over to kiss Lumina's cheek. "Be assured he will keep me safe.

"Safe as a crow in a gutter," he grinned.

Lumina left the eld woman to her somewhat dubious safety. She made her way through the marketplace hand in hand with the Goblin King, the silver cat perched happily on her shoulder.

The Keep soon loomed up ahead. They crossed over the bridge with its river of silvered clouds, and through the courtyard, the moon and stars beneath their feet.

They walked together through the golden hall, to the small door behind the throne. It was there the Goblin King stopped.

"Would you forgive me, my lady if I left you to go on without me from here?" he asked, his thumb brushing her knuckles with the lightest of caresses. "It will only be for a short while."

"Of course," she said, and with a small bow, he left.

She continued on through the bronze door, making her way down the sweeping staircase of the inverted tower. Once at the bottom, she lifted the key out from where she kept it next to Ember's ashes. Fitting it to the lock, she took a deep breath and turned.

It turned easily, unlocking with a soft click. Gently pushing open the door, she stepped through, pulling it closed quietly behind her. She stood once more in the golden glow of the door lantern. The heady scent of eglantine wrapped around her and there beneath it was a softer, more subtle scent; one that was very familiar to her.

Growing, one either side of her, were the roses she had planted when last she had been in the garden. Their canes, now tall and numerous, were covered in pale pink and raspberry-colored blossoms. Arching high over the doorway, they had entwined themselves with the branches of the door's petrified sentinels.

Pride filled Lumina. She stroked their petals and leaves, sharing her joy with them at how much they had grown. The roses shivered with happiness at her touch, raining petals down on both her and the silver cat as he sat grooming himself at her feet. She set off into the waiting darkness, a smile on her lips and rose petals in her hair.

Beyond the golden light, the garden had not changed since she last had been there. The pale white pillars and flagstone still stuck up from the barren earth like bleached bones. But for some reason, Lumina no longer saw despair in its bleakness, but a stark beauty and a potential that lay sleeping beneath the surface. With the tiny pine seedling still cupped safely in her hand, she set off down a path at random, trusting that she would come to a place that would suit her needs.

Above her, the moon shone silver-white in a black velvet sky. The path she followed wound and wound, finally bringing her up a rise to the top of a lone hill.

It was an empty place, the most desolate that she had yet seen in the garden. If garden it could be called, as she had yet to see any end to it. She was learning that distances here could be very deceiving. Despite all that, she smiled. It was easy for her to imagine the seedling here on this hill top, grown into a tall, stately tree. Daisies and tall grasses spreading out beneath his far reaching branches.

Decision made, Lumina knelt down and dug her hand into the soil. It was poor and dry, falling back into the hole almost as quickly as she scrapped it out. But she was not worried; the child of Old Father Pine had an indomitable will to grow. As soon as she placed the seedling in the hole she had made, she could feel the little roots reach down into the earth, nestling in as if they had just come home.

The silver cat, who had been watching all of this with very little interest, turned his head to look back the way they had come. He squeezed his eyes shut in a cat smile, a soft purr rumbling in his throat.

Lumina turned to see the Goblin King walking up the path, his starlight hair resplendent beneath the moon's caress. He stopped next to where she still knelt beside the now foot tall sapling. The little tree had sprouted a trio of branches that swayed softly even though no breeze blew.

"He looks happy," he said, kneeling down next to her, heedless of the dust and his fine coat. "I would not have thought he would thrive in such thin soil. It is your touch that brings life to this place," he said, turning and smiling at her with admiration.

"He is determined to grow," she said.

"So he is," the Goblin King agreed.

"I need more seeds," Lumina said, staring out at the barren plain.

"You will have them," he promised, offering her his hand.

Lumina took it and stood. Together, they followed the path as it wound down the other side of the hill. Eventually it led them between two monstrous pillars and down a broad set of stairs to a large sunken garden paved in brilliant white flagstones. Covered colonnades lined both sides of the garden, silent fountains hidden within their shadowy alcoves. Walled beds and bare patches of earth formed patterns centering on a long reflection pool which formed a perfect mirror for the starry sky above. Standing at its edge was a statue of the white stag.

"Oh," Lumina exclaimed. "I didn't know that there was more than one in the garden!"

"There is only the one," he assured her.

"Does he move then?" she asked.

"Not as you would think," he said. "It would be simpler to look upon the garden as you would a person's heart; some things are constant, while others change and grow."

"How sad that would be if this truly was a reflection of a person's heart," she said, taking in the barren earth and dead stones all around her.

Lorne could not help but agree as he watched Lumina walk away. She went to the pool's edge near where the stag stood. Kneeling down, she leaned out over the star filled water.

"Still, she continued, "there is a kind of beauty to it; subtle, yet beguiling in its nature." Reaching out, she lightly brushed her fingertips over the stag's reflection.

He felt a small smile pull at his lips as he made his way over to where she sat. Folding his legs tailor fashion, he settled down on the ground close to her.

"I am glad you think so," he said, reaching into his coat and retrieving the gift he had bought for her at the market. "And I hope that you will continue to bring life to it."

When she sat back to look at him, he took her hand and turned it over, placing the small soapstone box in her palm. She raised the lid, a joyous smile lighting up her face as she looked down at the two pearly seeds nestled in their mossy bed.

"They are beautiful!" she sang.

She was on her feet in an instant. As he watched, she went over to a large garden bed. It was close to the edge of the pool, and empty as they all were. Taking one of the seeds from its box, she planted it in the very middle of the bare earth. She had no sooner covered it, when a little green shoot began pushing its way up through the soil.

That done, she leapt gracefully over the still water to a matching bed on the other side. Once there, she planted the other seed as she had the first. It too, quickly pushed its way up out of the dark earth. She bent to kiss the tender green leaves, and in a thrice, the tiny seedling was a sapling, standing as tall as the sprite.

She leapt back across the water and did the same to the first. It too grew as though years had passed in the blink of an eye. Lorne could almost see the shadows of the trees they would become, blossom filled branches reaching out to each other across the water, intertwining like two lovers holding hands. He smiled at the vision.

Lumina came back to sit near him, her face shining as she watched the two trees. Her unreserved joy brought to mind happier times, which in turn set him to thinking of the reason that she now sat with him in this desolate garden.

"How is the boy faring?" he asked, only to see a shadow dim her shining face.

"I think the food and goat's milk have done him good," she said. "But, I fear his mind is broken. And I am afraid that it may not be possible to make it whole again."

The silver cat came seemingly out of nowhere to drape himself across his mistress's feet. Lorne watched her reach down to stroke the cat's ears, deriving comfort from his presence.

She was right to fear for the boy's mind. That he could not take her fear away bothered him more than he had expected.

"His mind will never be as it was," he said gently. "What protection my brother and I may have inherited from our mother's blood will be of almost no help to the boy. That blood runs too thinly in him."

"Perhaps, when he returns to his people, they will be able to help," she said, turning to look at him. Her golden gaze, so full of hope, was entrancing.

"He cannot return to his people," he said, unable to look away, trapped as fast as any fly in the amber of her eyes. "Time is not the same there as it is here. His people may have turned to dust long ago, or they may have yet to realize that he is missing, in which case they will think him mad when he tells them where he has been.

No matter which is true, he would no longer do well in the mortal realm. He can now see things that others cannot, and he always will. They will shun him for it as they did the eld woman. They may even kill him, if they fear him enough."

"Then he can come here," she said, but there was hesitation in her voice. Something furtive that set him to wondering what further games the Fairy Queen might be playing.

"It would be no better for him here than in the queen's court, I fear," he said, shaking his head. "Though we may be two courts, they both still reside in faerie."

"Then he can live with us in the glade," she said resolutely, her brows drawing together, like clouds before the storm.

Her determination made him want to smile. Though mild by nature, she was fierce in her desire to protect those she cared for. Again, it bothered him that in this too, he could do nothing to help her.

"Human children are not kittens, Lumina," he said gently. "They have neither claws nor fur and they do not survive well without shelter."

"Then why save him at all? If he will die either way, then let him do so in the fantasy the Fairy Queen has woven for him," she said, her voice catching. He stared in wonder as the tears filled her eyes, spilling like a river of diamonds down the silk of her cheek.

"Are you crying, Lumina?" he asked, reaching out to capture one. "Are you crying at the thought of the boy losing his life?"

She did not answer him, but he could see the truth in her eyes.

"Ah, my sweet lovely sprite, you amaze me so!" he said, truly astounded. "You who have never carried the burden of mortality; have, in fact, no true concept of death, yet still you felt the need to save a tiny kitten as he lay dying. And now, you cry for the sake of one mad little boy." He brought the crystal tear to his lips, the hopelessness tasting almost as sweet as honey on his tongue. "I have known what it is to be mortal. And I understand what it means to fear death; although it has been long years since I felt such things. Yet your compassion is much greater than my own." He reached out his hand out to cup her cheek, feeling her settle just a little into his touch.

"I *need* to save this boy because his blood obligates me to, and to leave him with the Fairy Queen would give her a power over me that I do not wish her to have," he said, stroking another tear away with his thumb. "I *want* to save him because you want him saved."

She closed her eyes, shuttering her heart from his gaze, leaving her thoughts a mystery to him.

"Stay with me," he said carefully. "Just the night. You need not even leave the garden if you do not wish to. I am sure it has already made a place for you to stay. In the morning, I will have something that should help protect the boy's mind."

The silver cat laying at her feet rubbed his cheek against his mistress's toes.

"I think it is a great idea, Mistress," the silver cat purred, looking over slyly and giving him a wink that made him second guess his invitation. "Who knows what familiar faces we will see here."

Lumina took the Goblin King's hands when he offered them, allowing him to draw them both to their feet.

"Do you really think that you can help the boy?" she asked.

"What I can do, I will," he promised.

They continued on through the sunken garden to a set of narrow stairs at the far end. At the top of them the path continued, eventually taking them to the heart of the garden. The statue of the white stag was absent of course, but the dancer still stood at the end of all paths, frozen in her endless dance. They passed her by, starting down another path just beyond.

It was a twisted thing that soon led them into what looked like a large copse of tall trees. They stood close together, straight and smooth-boled. Lumina reached out curiously as she passed, running her fingers along their silver-gray trunks and finding them velvety-soft to the touch, but just as lifeless as the two sentinels at the garden's door.

Lights twinkling in the branches above soon revealed themselves to be a multitude of many-hued lanterns dangling from the ends of slender chains, like strange jewel-toned fruit. They glowed warmly in the soft dark.

Deeper and deeper into the copse they went until they reached its very heart. There the surrounding trees made a roof of their branches; a small bower where the lanterns hung low and in great profusion, filling the small space with their gentle light. It reminded her in some ways of the den she and the silver cat shared in the winter, beneath the roots of Old Father Pine. Though honestly, she would be hard pressed to say why.

The place was strangely beautiful, filled with all sorts of curiosities. A large mirror, framed in burnished gold, stood on feet of alabaster, next to a vanity laid out with combs and brushes made of bone and shell. In the very middle of the bower was a large bed. Posts of golden jasper twined round with silver vines rose up from its four corners, holding aloft a canopy of gossamer curtains the color of peridots. Across the bed lay a velvet coverlet like a blanket of new spring grass.

"Does it suit, my lady?" asked the Goblin King.

"It does," Lumina assured him.

"I am glad. Rest well then, and let your heart be at peace. Nothing will bother you here," he said bowing slightly. "I'll return once I have what is needed."

With a final farewell, he left them, and soon disappeared from sight amongst the petrified trees.

Lumina sat on the bed, after the Goblin King had left. The silver cat jumped up beside her, mincing his way across the springy surface.

"What do you think, Mistress?" he asked as he made his way to the head of the bed.

"I think it is all so strange," she said with a sigh. "In some ways, it is just as the Fairy Queen said it would be, barren and desolate. And there is no doubt that the night, not the day, reigns supreme here. Yet despite all that, I am still drawn to it, like a moth to a flame."

"I meant, what do you think about the bed?" he said. She looked back over her shoulder to find him on one of the pillows, watching her with sleepy eyes. His paws kneaded happily, one then the other with a soothing regularity that was almost hypnotic.

"Of course you did," she said with a smile, finally laying down herself. She slipped beneath the covers onto sheets as soft as rose petals. She turned to face the silver cat on the pillow next to hers. Even that was odd, as she was the one usually tucked in next to his head when they slept, not the other way round.

As she lay there, she could almost feel the silence. It surrounded her, growing heavier with each breath. Until a soft sound nudged at her ears; a gentle purr that grew louder and louder till it seemed to fill the whole of the garden. The ebb and flow of it was soothing, like a heartbeat. Her mind settled as her breathing matched its steady cadence. It drew her in deeper and deeper until she was drifting in that between time. The time that comes just before true sleep claims you.

Another sound found her as she floated in that soft place. A fiddle's tune, as familiar to her as the silver cat's purr, wound its way through the gentle throb. She wondered where the fiddler was, in his great black coat, cold white fires burning deep in the bottomless depths of his eyes, as he spun the world round with his playing. It pulled at her, compelling and seductive, drawing her from her bed.

The silver cat must have been exhausted because not a whisker twitched when she slipped quietly from beneath the covers. She ran lightly down the paths, the music beckoning her on. It led her through the garden door and up the whorled staircase, not stopping until she had reached the little bronze door at the very top. She placed her ear to the cool metal. The fiddler was there, just on the other side. She opened the door slowly, peering furtively around its edge.

The hall opened up before her, golden and bright. Dancers filled its jasper floors, swirling between the agate pillars. The whole of her vision was consumed by them as they gamboled past. Their vague features smudged and undefined, were revealed only in flashes, a kaleidoscope of pictures falling like leaves before her eyes: a donkey's nose, an ox's horns, a fox's tail, a raven's eye. Some had faces like angels, others were as wrinkled as old trees. The goblins laughed and cried and belled and roared as they danced to the fiddler's wild tune.

The music pulled at Lumina's feet. Still she hesitated, until she saw from the corner of her eye a pair of coat-tails, dark as a crow's wing, flutter by. She left her hiding place then, letting the door close quietly behind her.

She slipped through the dancers as they frolicked and twirled, pulled along by the hint of a dusky sleeve or flash of obsidian feather. Yet, try as she might, her quarry stayed just beyond her. Oddly, the dancers took no notice of her as she wove through them. Stranger still, there was no brush of fabric across her skin as she passed between them, no feel of fur, nor of scale either. As if they were ghosts, or maybe she was. Perhaps even now her body still lay curled up in the middle of a stone wood on a bed of thistledown and silk.

The tune swelled, and she turned to find the fiddler there behind her. But he was not the one she had expected. It was not Crow, but the Goblin King who stood there, playing a familiar fiddle as he smiled down at her.

It was then that she knew that sleep had truly found her. So she let the music claim her, since it was only a dream, joining the dancers' merry reel. Each touch revealed a different face, as she was whisked from one to the other, until she found herself in the arms of the Goblin King. Smiling up at him as he spun her around, telling her he loved her in a voice that was not his own.

Lumina's eyes fluttered open to find a ceiling of stony branches laced above her behind a canopy of green gossamer. She rolled over to find the silver cat still curled up in the pillow next to her. Stretched out on the bed just beyond him, was the Goblin King.

"Good morning," he said, a gentle smile on his lips. "Did you dream well?"

Uncertainty sluiced through Lumina's belly, making her question whether her dream of dancing in the goblin's revels had truly been just a dream. But the Goblin King's voice was his own again. He no longer spoke with another's, saying words that had never before been spoken.

"Ummm yesss, wonderful dreams," said the silver cat, stretching his toes. The end of his tail flipped itself out to lay across the Goblin King's cheek. "Of chasing crows through autumn woods and bowls of cream for breakfast."

"Then go and eat, you insolent thing," the Goblin King said, his soft gaze never leaving Lumina's. "The second part of your dream sits on the table over there."

The silver cat stood up, stretched some more, then leapt lightly over Lumina and off the bed.

She made to follow, but the Goblin King reached out, covering her hand with his.

"Stay a while, sweet sprite," he said. "I have brought what I promised. Something that may offer some protection for our mad little boy."

He slid his hand away from hers slowly, like a wave retreating over the sand. The tips of his fingers coming to rest against hers, revealing a pendant that now lay in the palm of her hand. It was a crystal vial wrapped in a filigree of burnished gold. The workmanship was not unlike the ring Crow had given her, but instead of ravens amongst the roses, the pendant was of stags leaping free of brambles.

"It would be best if he drank it, but if he ate something made from it, that should suffice," he said.

Lumina sat up and the Goblin King did so as well. Holding the pendant up, she turned it this way and that. Inside was a liquid that shone like garnets in the lantern's light.

"What is it?" she asked.

"A few drops of my blood," he replied.

"Your blood!"

"Yes. But there is no reason to fear," he reassured her. "It will do the boy no harm and hopefully a great deal of good."

But Lumina's horror had more to do with what someone could do with a few drops of the Goblin King's blood, and less to do with any harm she thought it would bring to the boy.

"This is a dangerous thing. And a great deal of trust that you are placing in me. There is much someone could do with this," she said, knowing the Fairy Queen would turn the seasons backwards to possess what Lumina now held in her hand. "I have not given you a reason to place such trust in me."

"Yet, you have it all the same," he said, taking the necklace from her hand, and slipping it over her head, the pendant coming to rest just above her heart. Her hand came up to cover it.

"I trust your heart," he said, his hand coming up to cover hers.

Lumina wished she could say as much.

It was a dreary gray day when next the Fairy Queen brought the boy to visit Lumina. A thick blanket of clouds covered the sky, washing all the color from the world. The misty rain did not encourage them to wander. So they sat beneath the sheltering branches of Old Father Pine, in the same tiny dell which had up till recently housed his progeny.

Lumina sat across from the Fairy Queen, who had forgone the guise of the doe-eyed cherub she usually wore for that of a buxom young woman with flaxen hair and pale blue eyes. Her skin was the color of milk, and roses bloomed on her round cheeks, in a merry sort of way. She looked much like the milkmaid Lumina had seen when she had last visited the farmhouse.

The boy sat between them, and before them burned a fire, though there was no fuel to feed it. Salamanders cavorted in the flames, called there by the Fairy Queen. One among their number was familiar to Lumina and when the queen's eye was somewhere else, he winked at her. His body twisted and swayed towards her in the steps of a dance they had long danced together. Then he leapt back with the others to frolic for the queen's pleasure. At that moment, it occurred to Lumina that she could call Ember away from the flames if she chose to, despite the queen's whim which held him there. That revelation was both thrilling and puzzling, and made her wonder what it meant that she could have such influence.

The Fairy Queen had seemed somewhat distracted since she arrived. Her wide blue eyes searched about them as though she expected something to be there that wasn't. Finally, she turned her attention back to Lumina.

"Has Lorne been here recently?" the queen asked her.

"Not for some time," she answered truthfully, for it had indeed been some time since the Goblin King had come to the glade.

"Strange," the queen said with a shiver. "It feels as though he is standing right beside me!" Without looking, she reached out to stroke the arm of the boy who sat next to her. "Sing something for us, my dove. Perhaps it will chase away this miasma." At her command, the boy began to sing with a voice as sweet as a siren's.

The wind whispered through the needles above them, sending a soft shower of rain drops down on their heads that no one paid any mind to, not even the boy. Never once did he reach up to wipe away the drops as they ran down his face. He continued to sing, even as they slid over his eyes and across his lips. Nothing else seemed to exist in his world at that moment save for the wishes of his queen.

What the Goblin King had said to her as they sat under the cherry trees gnawed at her. Faerie might not be a place where the boy could stay, but the mortal realm no longer held a place for him either.

Thoughts of the Goblin King made her want to reach for the pendant that lay warm on her chest, pulsing softly in time with her own heart. Instead she placed a hand on the large bundle next to her.

"What do you have there?" the Fairy Queen asked, her gaze intent. "Is it the apple from the witch's garden?"

"It is," Lumina confirmed.

"Well done!" the queen exclaimed. "And was it the last one?"

"It was," said Lumina, regret weighing heavy on her heart, some of which must have shown in her face, for the Fairy Queen was quick to reassure her.

"Don't lose heart, little sister," the queen said, mistaking Lumina's regret for despair. "It will not be you who weds the Goblin King. When all that you gather for me is put in a certain way, he will happily wed another in your stead. You will not be forsworn and you will be free. And it will all be of his choosing."

"And what of the boy?" Lumina asked.

"He will go to the Goblin King's court, as I have promised, as page to his new queen."

For some reason, Lumina did not find that as reassuring as it should have been. In fact, she found the thought of the Goblin King marrying someone else, even willingly, a troubling one.

Even so, when the Fairy Queen left, it never occurred to Lumina not to give her the apple.

CHAPTER 12

Lady of the Glade

Lumina sat in the cool October sun, the silver cat a warmth curled up at her back. She watched with interest as the glade around her and the lake meadow beyond were inundated with activity.

The day before, the Goblin King had brought with him a circle of loireag to spin her wedding dress. Diminutive and plain, but with voices to rival the angels, they sang as they set about their task.

Down near the lake's edge, Meg sat with her charge, milking the old nanny goat and sharing it out with the loireag, then brushing her down with twists of grass. The gruagach seemed content in her work.

"I wonder at the Fairy Queen's tolerance of so many goblins in her wood," Lumina said to her companion, who sat a short distance away, stringing his fiddle.

"What of it?" said Crow. "They are here at your sufferance, not hers."

"*My* sufferance? I am not sure why such a thing would matter," she said without rancor. "I am only a small piece in this greater game. And I am not sure I am even the most important one."

Crow stood up, and came to kneel in front of her. "You, my sweet sprite, hear the music of the world and sing life into that which needs it," he said, reaching out to take both her hands in his. "Here, in this place, you can be as you want to be. Try. Try something which you have only done by someone else's power."

Lumina thought of when she danced in Underhill, and when she walked through the Goblin King's Keep. How tall she had stood. How the silver cat would ride on her shoulder. And from one heartbeat to the next the earth fell away, and she stood high above the golden grasses.

Crow stood in front of her, taller still.

"You are the Lady of the Glade," he said, letting go of her hands to cup her face with his graceful talons. "And you are much greater than you know."

Five days ago the boy had come to the glade unexpectedly, and strangely, alone. He had come to Lumina, and called her 'Mistress' in a voice like a mad angel. At first, he would not eat as he usually did. But as the day began to wane, she was able to finally get him to drink honeyed milk into which she had poured the Goblin King's blood.

He ate for her then, and stroked the silver cat who had laid in his lap. When the sun had set and the amethyst hues of twilight painted the sky, she led him back to the door to Underhill. A light shone through the cleft in the boulder and inside dancers could be seen spinning amongst the trunks of the crystal trees.

A smile lit the boy's face as they headed towards the beckoning sound of music and laughter. Watching him, her chest grew tight. His smile was peaceful and angelic.

But then, for the briefest moment as the boy looked back at her, she saw his eyes fill with uncertainty and despair. They seemed to plead with her, though for what she did not know. Then he stepped through the door.

Now, Lumina sat perched on one of Swift's antlers, the empty vial glittering in the light of the newly risen moon, shining like a star in the palm of her hand.

She had quickly grown used to its pulsing warmth nestled over her heart. Now that it was gone, she was surprised at how much she missed it, wondering when it was that it had become something dear to her.

She leaned her head against the tine next to her, looking out to the horizon where the harvest moon sat, huge and golden, in the soft night sky. She was no longer sure if saving the boy would be the kindness she had meant it to be.

The boy was not the only one troubling her thoughts; the Goblin King plagued them as well. She wondered sometimes if he had put a glamour on her, for she found herself enchanted by him and increasingly comfortable in his company. If it was a glamour, then why did the thought of marrying him still make her feel that if she were to do so, she would lose something very dear to her?

The moon gave her no answers.

She turned her gaze earthward to find a familiar dark figure sitting on the antler opposite hers. He was watching her patiently, one long leg stretched out between the tines, his hands clasping the knee of the other. She had not heard him arrive, but a great heaviness lifted from her at the sight of him.

"Crow," she sighed softly, her relief ghosting from her lips.

"Good evening, fair one. A fine night isn't it?" he said, gesturing at the golden moon.

"A beautiful night," she agreed, her earlier thoughts seemed much less troubling now. "Have you come to play for me? It is a perfect night for such things."

"So it is," he said. "It is also the perfect night to collect what you need from the Well of Stars. If you still wish to do so, that is?"

"I do," she said with more conviction than she would have had a moment before.

"Then we should be on our way, before the night gets much older," said Crow although he made no move to stand. "Where is the silver cat?"

"Off hunting," Lumina replied. "Though I cannot say whether that means he is out chasing down small creatures or charming the eld woman out of a bowl of cream."

Crow laughed. "Then it seems we are on our own."

"Is Hoax not with you?" she asked, noticing the distinct lack of a silver-tongued phooka.

"No, tonight is Samhain, so he is off filling his belly with the last of the year's apples and tricking the foolish into taking him for a ride," he answered. "Should we ask our friend Swift to carry us?"

"I would gladly take you to wherever you so wished, dear one" Swift said, having not missed the conversation taking place just above his ears.

"No, my gallant," she said fondly. With the harvest came the roaring of the stags, a time when Swift would defend his family from all comers. That he would offer to take her at this time was a testament to his affection for her. "I think we will use our own feet."

She slipped from his antlers. Her feet reached the earth even as her arms were still around the stag's neck. She pressed her cheek into his warm coat happily. Though it was not the first time she had done such a thing since Crow had shown her that she could, it was still new enough that the wonder of it had not worn off.

Laughing, she spun away, gamboling out into the night. A taloned-tipped hand clasped hers, twirling her into a familiar embrace. Together they waltzed across the meadow to the bank of the stream. Hand in hand, they skipped lightly across the stones to the other side, where the goblin's wood enfolded them in its dark embrace.

The air beneath the trees was lighter than it was usually wont to be, their ever-present whisperings more like sighs and soft promises shared by lovers in the deep of the night. She and Crow walked companionably through the wood, and despite the uncertainty of her errand, Lumina's heart was light, her hand comfortable in the clasp of the one who held it.

The dell was shrouded in darkness when they reached it, the moon still a ways off from its zenith, denying them the joy of her light. Lumina let go Crow's hand, stepping up to the crumbling stones that once towered so far above her head, which now stood not even as high as her hip. The joy she had felt dimmed slightly in the face of her task.

"What is wrong, fair one?" he asked softly from where he waited so close behind her. "Have you changed your mind?" The breath of his question was a caress across her cheek. She thought she heard a whisper of regret in his voice. Or was it hope? Lumina could not tell, and as with all things concerning Crow and the Goblin King, she could not bring herself to ask.

"No," she answered, firming her resolve, letting her doubts fall away, at least for the time being.

"Then pluck a rose, Lumina, thorns and all. Throw it in the well, and hold tight the vial that rests over your heart."

She did as he bade her do, never once wondering how he knew about the pendant she wore. When next she opened her hand she found the vial was no longer empty. What swirled inside was both light and dark, all colors and none.

"What I am doing, is it wrong?" she wondered aloud. "Am I betraying the promise I made?"

Crow pulled her back into his embrace, wrapping her in stillness, his arms a shield against doubt. He laid his cheek atop her head.

"You betray no one," he whispered adamantly, his beak sliding across her hair. "I doubt you ever could."

Crow had left Lumina beneath the wild rose long after midnight, while she still danced with Ember. Now he sat in the branches of Old Father Pine, keeping vigil while she slept. Tiny once again, she lay curled up next to the silver cat, softly lit by the glow of the salamander's fire.

Hoax was perched on the branch beside him.

"You know, I think I may agree with the salamander; you should tell her," the phooka said, ruffling his feathers and settling in for what he knew from experience would be a long wait. "If you don't, I might."

"Would you, I wonder?" said Crow, his eyes not leaving the sleeping sprite below. "Would you go against me for her sake?"

The phooka scoffed. "It's not going against you, so much as going around you, and I do that all the time just for fun."

"True enough," said Crow. "And I know that you are right, my friend. I should tell her. I want to tell her, but after all this time, I am not sure how to."

"Straight forward would be the best way, I think."

"So says the lord of tricksters."

Hoax bowed his head and spread his wings, genuflecting in acknowledgment.

"Still," the phooka continued, "is letting her continue on with this game the Fairy Queen plays a good idea?"

"Perhaps not, but I am afraid it is the only way to find out what the end game is."

The Hart's Dance

"Inch worm, inch worm, do not rest.
Measure me for my wedding dress.
Make it of thistledown and cobweb lace,
with jewels of dew t' shine in the moon's bright face..."

The loireags' sweet voices floated on the wind as they went about the task of making Lumina's wedding dress. Throughout the glade and into the meadow beyond, tall grasses and bare branches had been transformed into looms filled with shimmering spider-silk and cloud-white thistledown.

"Merry lord, fairy lord, sing your green song.
Quiet we'll fly over wood and lawn.
Underhill, overhill, through briar and thorn
Promise to come to me before the bright dawn."

In the center of all this industry stood Lumina, standing well above the heavy headed grasses.

"Hold your arms up Mistress," said one of the weavers, dropping a bundle of cloth over them once Lumina had done so.

It felt like a cool breeze and shimmered like starlight as it passed over Lumina's head. The weaver's eyes were bright with happiness as she fussed with the folds of the dress.

"Oh Mistress! You will look absolutely lovely!" she said, her voice filled with the satisfaction of a job well done.

"Yes, she will," a voice said from behind Lumina.

Lumina looked over her shoulder to see the queen of the fairies coming from out of the trees' shadows. She did not wear the guise of a little girl this time, nor that of the milkmaid either. The shape she wore was of a woman in her prime, round-hipped and smooth-shouldered. Her hair was the bright copper and gold of autumn leaves, and she had eyes like pale green beryls.

The little weaver froze for a moment, then quickly bent, her little hands swiftly gathering up the folds of fabric in preparation for pulling it back over Lumina's head.

"Be still little one," the Fairy Queen said to the weaver. "Your work looks lovely where it is; leave it. I will only be a moment. You can go back to your work."

The queen's dismissal was clear, but the loireag looked at Lumina, who smiled at her, before she curtsied and headed back to where the others were weaving.

The Fairy Queen looped her arm through Lumina's as though they were sisters in truth, and began to walk down towards the lake shore. Lumina had no choice but to follow.

The reeds and rushes were golden along the path they walked. The cool wind gathered up their fluffy seeds and sent them spinning and dancing through the air around them. The endless lavender-blue sky above them brought unbidden to her mind thoughts of the Goblin King's hall, with its ceiling of chalcedony and pillars of golden agate.

"I see that preparations for the wedding are coming along well. Are you having second thoughts?" the Fairy Queen speculated. A swift stab of pain shot through Lumina's heart like a needle.

"I have questioned whether such a fate would really be so bad," Lumina admitted since the queen had asked her outright and she was not a creature to lie. "Still, I have brought what you asked for," she said, pulling the chain which held the crystal vial from around her neck. She paused for a moment, reluctant to part with it.

"All is well, little sister," the queen assured her, misunderstanding the reason for her reluctance. "The choice you are making is the best one."

The Fairy Queen took the necklace from her, holding it up so that it spun and glittered in the light of the sun.

"What a beautiful thing!" she said mesmerized by the vial and what it held. "Where did you get it?"

"From the Goblin King," Lumina admitted.

The Fairy Queen stopped, forcing Lumina to stop with her. "Does he know what you have used it for?" she asked, her voice carefully neutral.

"No," Lumina replied, wondering what he would think if he did know.

"Ahh, good," the Fairy Queen sighed, as they resumed walking. "All would have been lost if you had. There is still one more piece we need. It is just a small thing. There is a garden sheltered deep within the goblin's Keep, the

Queen's Garden it is called. I need the key to that garden. He must give it to you without you asking, but I have no doubts that he soon will. When he does, bring it to me."

Lumina closed her eyes. "Such a small thing," she said softly to herself. This could be done now, yet she made no move to give her the key that hung heavily at her hip.

"Just that one more thing, a small thing," the Fairy Queen assured her. "Take heart! We are so close, and soon it will all be done. I will warn you though, have a care to never let his lips touch yours. Never! Should he kiss you, or you him for that matter, it would bring ruin. And I fear that all you care for would suffer."

Lumina nodded her head and promised to be careful.

The queen left shortly thereafter, leaving Lumina alone with her thoughts. The foremost in her mind was the key that she wasn't sure she could part with, and that the thought of the Goblin King marrying another still did not bring the relief that it should.

Gray clouds had blown in, covering the sun. There was no one working the looms now. The gossamer fabric which had shone in the light only a short time ago, now looked spectral and ominous, like shrouds for the dead.

Lumina closed the garden door behind her, and looked out over the Queen's Garden, her garden. She had visited many times since she first brought the little pine tree here to grow just after the autumn equinox. Now, with Hollentide Eve nearly here, she marveled at the changes wrought in only a little over a month's time.

The roses at the door had grown tall, taller than any of their kind in the mortal realm. Their arching canes intertwined with the stone branches above, still heavy with blossoms, making a sweet-scented bower.

Beyond the golden pool of light in which she stood, the garden was awash in silver. There was no barren earth here now. The pillars that once rose like old bones were covered in moonflower and honeysuckle. Night-blooming jasmine arched over the stone walls. Bellflowers bloomed along the walks, glowing like little lanterns of sapphire and amethyst. And in between the path's stones, moss grew starry eyed with tiny white flowers. Everywhere there were growing things. Most were from seeds she herself had brought, but not all. The Goblin King had seemed to take great pleasure in gifting her with seeds from all over the earth, and some not from the mortal world at all.

She walked out along the paths. She could feel how the garden had changed, and it was no longer silent. A wind breathed a joyous sigh through the garden, setting the flowers to dancing. So Lumina danced too. Throughout the garden she danced, past fountains that were no longer silent, beneath the branches of trees that were both heavy with fruit and covered with blossoms, for the seasons held no sway here. The wind pulled at the blooms, twining them in her hair, making it a night sky filled with rainbows and stars. She in turn wove a garland of roses as she went and when she found the statue of the white stag, she crowned his antlers with it before spinning out into the place where all the paths met.

Around and around she danced, and the wind danced with her. She spun and she leapt. Strong, slender hands replaced the wind as her partner, holding her aloft.

The Goblin King flowed into the dance as if he had been a part of it all along. There were no measured steps nor set course as there had been when they danced on Midsummer's Eve. Together, apart, together again, inevitably drawn back to each other. Spinning, leaping, hair intertwined like strands of starlight through a night sky. Moving as one with him, she danced as she had not since she had last danced with another, on the crumbling stones of an old well filled with stars and dreams.

As they whirled past, she saw that the stag had moved out of the shadows to stand in front of the statue of the dancer, whose arms were now encircled about his neck. When next Lumina saw him, he was no longer a stag, but the image of Lorne himself, garbed only in starlight and the flowers she herself had bedecked him in. His lips only a breath apart from those of the dancer's.

The world seemed to spin faster and faster. She was elated. She was unsteady. She felt as though she was both trapped and flying at the same time.

Hidden in the shadows at the edge of the circle was another statue, with a crow's beaked visage and tattered coattails carved from jet. Her heart stuttered in her chest.

She looked up into the face of the Goblin King. He was so close, his lips beautiful and full of promises. The shadow of the dark statue loomed over her shoulder while the Fairy Queen's warning screamed through her mind.

"No," she breathed, and with that single word the spell the dance had woven shattered around them. She stepped out of the Goblin King's embrace, finally understanding the reason why reluctance had always plagued her at the thought of marrying him.

"I cannot give you my love when it belongs to another," she said, the words wrenching at her soul. Unwilling to hear what he might say, she flew from him.

Lorne made no move to stop her as the sprite fled from the garden.

He turned his gaze to the statues at the center of the circle. Where once only two stood, there now stood three. To one side was the image of the Goblin King and to the other was Crow. The dancer stood between them, her hands covering her face as though she wept.

He sighed deeply.

"She says she loves another, huh? So now what should I do?" he asked no one in particular.

The tableau before him changed. The statue in its tattered coattails made of jet now stood with the Mask of Crows in his taloned hand. The face he revealed was none other than Lorne's own.

"Of course, as I should have done long ago, and would have done, had I not been a coward."

That fool of a phooka had been right.

Out across the moors Lumina ran, alone beneath the endless blue sky. Yet even its vastness seemed small compared to the realization that she had just come to.

She loved Crow.

All the doubts and misgivings that she had felt fell away in the face of that truth. Did the Fairy Queen not say plainly that Lorne would marry another by his own choice? That the boy would still go into his care once he wed. She wished to see Crow; her desire and hope that he would be in the glade lent wings to her feet. Either that, or the land had folded in on itself, for she arrived in her glade in much less time than it should have taken.

It was not Crow who greeted her in the glade, but rather the Fairy Queen, waiting in all her ethereal glory. No mortal guise clothed her this time; reality bent around her beauty, making the mortal realm look flat and crude by comparison. And when Lumina approached her, a terrible compassion lit her face.

"Child, what is wrong?" she asked, but the knowledge that shone in her eyes made Lumina believe that she already knew.

Lumina did not trust the words that may pass through her lips. So, she lifted the key out from her spider-silk bag in silence, placing it in the queen's hand.

"Well done, child. Well done," the Fairy Queen said, her eyes alight with triumph.

"The Goblin King will not think my oath broken?"

Lumina asked seeking reassurances that her choice would bring no harm. "And the boy will be safe?"

The beauty of the smile that graced the queen's lips could bring even the heavens to its knees.

"Yes child, yes to all."

It was already well into the night when he finally reached the glade. All of this was beyond his understanding, so he had stopped at the eld woman's, and recieved a tongue-lashing for his trouble. He had thought that he had left Hoax behind him at the eld woman's house, but the shadow of a raven passing overhead told him that the phooka had not stayed there. Which was certainly no surprise.

He did not see the salamander's glow, nor did he see the pale shape of the silver cat, but he certainly saw the beautiful sprite who danced there beneath the light of the waning moon.

The life emanating from her called to him; his heart overflowed with it as it always did, pulling him into her orbit and holding him there as the earth to the moon. He watched her golden eyes fill with warmth when she felt his arms go around her, joining her in her dance. And he knew when she was going to kiss him, perhaps even before she herself did. His eyes stayed open as she reached up. He watched the confusion when her lips, expecting one thing, met his and found another.

Everything stopped, their dance at an end as he reached up and removed the Mask of Crows. He could see the pale reflection of himself in her wide golden eyes. Could see the emotions race across her face like clouds across the sun: surprise, joy, confusion, betrayal. His heart held on tightly to the joy he had seen.

She stepped back from him and he knew he stood on a precipice.

"Where is Crow?" she asked, but he saw the pieces falling into place, realization dawning even as she spoke. "Why did you never tell me? All this time, from the very beginning... and now..." As understanding grew, the look of betrayal that sat unnaturally on her lovely face turned to one of despair. Still his hands did not reach out, his feet did not carry him to her, any words that he might have said stayed frozen on his lips as though he were one of the statues in the Queen's Garden. And then she was gone, walking away into the night.

"Fool," said a familiar voice, and as the black horse walked past him, he felt the sting across his cheek as the phooka flicked his tail.

"That could have gone better," said the silver cat who now sat at his feet. "It is times like these, Master, when it is easy for me to believe you were once a mortal man."

His traitorous feet finally moved. They carried him none too quickly in the direction that his beloved and the phooka had taken.

CHAPTER 14

Consequences

She had no destination in mind when she walked away from the Goblin King, her eyes blind as her mind spiraled with her realization; the Goblin King and the creature she had come to love were one and the same, and she had betrayed them both.

She walked into something warm and solid, the phooka's dark hide seeming to have shaped itself from the night air in front of her. She found that she was in the circle of his neck, his brawny shoulder just in front of her.

"Mount on my back, fair one," he urged, nuzzling at her hip. "Let me carry you away for a short time."

Flinging herself astride his warm back, tangling her fingers in his mane, she let him carry her off into the darkness. Her tears fell freely, as unfettered as the phooka beneath her.

Eventually he brought her to the old well. There she slipped off his back, leaving him to stand alone, a shaggy black pony amongst the ever blooming forget-me-nots, as she went to sit on the crumbling stones.

"And who are you then, Hoax?" she asked.

"Your servant, as I told you once before, dearheart." There in the place of the shaggy pony was the tousle-haired goblin, sitting cross-legged in the ocean of flowers.

The very same one who had danced with her on Midsummer's eve and led her to her doom. Her heart was a void in her chest, as she felt her world fracture and crumble around her.

"I almost knew you, that day in the goblin market," she said.

"For a moment, I thought you had. I was sorry when you didn't," he said in all sincerity.

"Yet, you did not think to tell me? Or to hint, so that I might come to find the truth?"

"Surely I thought about it," he admitted. "But ultimately it was not my secret to tell. And as I am sure my master would be happy to tell you, I may not always be a truthful servant, but I am a loyal one. I have been even from the time before, when he was still a mortal man. Ever since I thought to take a certain lord's son for the ride of his life, only to have him surprise me with a halter over my head. I was the mount that bore him the day the Fairy Queen stole him away from mortal eyes, and the black horse he rode when Janet freed his brother from the Fairy Queen. And when she blinded and cursed him, I was the raven that rode in his antlers to guide him for more than a century. I have been his loyal knight for four more still. Now here is a truth that is mine to tell, one I will swear on my blood to; he loves you. He has since the night he saw you take pride in a half-dead kitten."

He stood up from where he was and came to kneel before her as though he truly were a supplicant before his queen.

"Never in all the centuries that I have known him

has he loved another as he loves you. Not even the Fairy Queen, who had his love for a time, but not the key to his heart. It has only ever been yours. It is a precious thing, Lady. It had been barren for so long, but your touch has made it grow again."

"If what you say is true, then my betrayal may be the greater of the two," she said, heart heavy with regret. "Carry me back home, Hoax."

When next she looked there was a black horse kneeling at her feet. She sat upon his back and he rose as if on springs. They headed back towards the glade and an uncertain future.

The unfamiliar scent of wood smoke was tickling her nose long before they reached the edge of the goblin's wood. Hoax leapt forward into a dead run before Lumina even had time to be concerned over the implications of what such a thing might mean. He cleared the wood's edge, and leapt the stream, only to land on the edge of a nightmare.

The trees of her glade were columns of fire. Fingers of flame ate away at the dry grasses of the meadow, and salamanders danced everywhere. Towering, sinuous figures writhing and leaping, laughing while Lumina's world burned.

She leapt down from Hoax's back as she pulled out the wooden box full of ashes which she upended, spilling the contents in a circle around her.

"Ember, come to me!" she commanded in a voice unlike her own, one which could not be denied.

No spark flew to her on the wind; there was no need. The fire was there before her. From it Ember stepped, now a towering figure whose height rivaled even the Goblin King's. He knelt before Lumina, his head bowed.

"My Lady, you have called me and I have come," he said in a voice of smoke and flame. "What would you have of me?"

"Cool the flames," she said, her will still adamant. "Send them back down into sleep."

"I don't know that I can," said the salamander. "This fire was fueled with power and that power courses through it still."

"Ember, my home is burning," she pleaded, desperation welling up.

The salamander turned to look at the fire, as if seeing it for the first time.

"What are you willing to do to save it?" he asked.

"Whatever I must," she answered.

"Will you dance in the flames with me?" His gaze was sharp as he asked, piercing her down to her very core. She did not flinch away.

"I will," she said, firm in her resolution despite the sound of protest coming from where Hoax stood behind her.

The salamander rose and offered her his hand, which she took without hesitation. Though her fingers were wreathed in flames, they did not hurt, but nor was it comfortable. It sat just on the edge of pain, but she would endure much worse to save all that she cared for.

"I am not sure what you will feel," the salamander

admitted, "but I know that as long as your hand is in mine, you will not truly burn."

He led her towards the wall of fire engulfing the meadows grasses.

"Lumina! Fair one, don't do this!" Hoax called out. "Call to your king and he will come."

But Lumina ignored him and walked with Ember into the flames.

For a moment, as she stepped into the fire, she burned. Pain lanced through her in that long heartbeat, and she could feel the scream trapped in her throat yet was unable to give it voice. Then the veil parted and before her was a land of wonder.

Towering spires of light filled a vague realm of ephemeral shades, and around them the salamanders danced. Beautiful, luminous beings with skin of the palest gold, swathed in crimson gossamer. So different from the creatures that she was used to seeing, cavorting through the fires. Motes of light rose into the air with every step they made, and around their feet, spirals of bright blossoms swirled out in whorls, only to shimmer and disappear.

She could feel the sway of Ember beside her, and when she turned her eyes to him she found him much changed as well. Next to her was a man with features as fine as any fairylord's. Eyes like two copper pennies shone from beneath hair the color of deepest garnet.

"I have always wanted to truly dance with you, my lady," he said, smiling down at her. "But you must lead this dance, for if I do, your home will continue to burn.

Lead and I will follow. Together, we will gather the flames until they only know our song."

For the first time since she came into being, she found that she could not dance. There were no songs tugging at her feet, just a building tension, a tingling anticipation like that which heralds a thunderstorm. She willed her feet to move into the silence.

With that first step, a wave of rapture washed over her, surrounding her, pulling her feet into a dance that left her breathless. She laughed joyously, and Ember held her close. They spun and whirled, caught up like leaves in a storm.

But Lumina quickly began to understand what the salamander had meant when he said that she must lead this dance. She did not slow her steps, nor did she try to tame the wildness that drew them along. Instead she danced faster, with greater abandon. Teasing, seducing, drawing all to her.

One by one, the spires of light left their places and gathered to her, the dancers fitting themselves to her song. Then they began to diminish, laughing happily as they became sparks on the wind, until only a single column of light was left. It surrounded Ember, infusing him so that his skin shone as bright as the sun. The world about them was only a vague dream now, filled with shadows and apparitions that meant nothing.

But they did mean something. The dance had come to its natural end. Ember's smile was forlorn, now that their dance was done. He bowed his head and she kissed his brow, extinguishing the light.

The veil parted and Lumina found that they were back at the place where they had first entered the flames. Both Ember's hands were in hers. But now his skin was the color of soot and his hair as white as ash. From top of head to bottom of foot, he was a colorless gray, like all the world around them. All but his eyes, which still burned like a banked fire.

"I understand now," she said. It was finally clear to her what the salamander had always meant when he said that he did not see the world as she did. As was the effort that he had put forth so that he could be a part of hers.

"Thank you, I am in your debt," she said, "but I am not sure I can pay the price you will ask."

"There can never be a debt between us. I am yours, a willing servant," he said. "There is a price, of course, but I am sure you will find it a small one."

With that he leaned forward and kissed her lips.

There was a flash of pain and she gasped. A burning seared its way down her throat as though she had swallowed a hot coal. She clutched her hands to her chest, but the heat quickly settled into a pleasant warmth that wrapped around her heart. She stared up at the salamander in wonder.

"Be still, fairylord," he said to someone who stood just beyond her sight, his eyes never leaving hers. "I have done no harm to your bride."

"Other than to kiss her," said Hoax's familiar voice. Lumina turned her head towards the speaker.

There at the edge of the destruction stood the phooka beside his master. Lorne, the Goblin King, still held the

Mask of Crows in his gauntleted hand. The spill of starlight hair down Crow's long coat seemed strange as he stood there in the dawn's silvery light. The morning breeze stirred the ash so that it swirled up between them like ghosts.

"There is no need now for ashes between us, my queen," said Ember, his warm breath brushing her ear as he whispered to her. "If ever you've need of me, speak my name and will me there, and on your next breath I will be at your side. From this moment until the end of forever, you hold a part of me within you. Never again need you fear the flames."

She turned her wide-eyed gaze back towards Ember as he straightened and stepped away from her. She watched as he became ashes himself, quickly drawn apart by the wind, save a single spark that was soon lost in the early morning light.

Lumina turned and walked away from where Lorne and Hoax stood. Looking around her, she tried to reconcile what she had seen in the realm of fire to the destruction that surrounded her.

Old Father Pine was scorched save for the highest branches. The wild rose, where they had made their home for so long, only a charred skeleton of blackened canes.

The soft sound of keening drew her on, past where the Rowan Maiden mourned against the stump of her tree. Her silver skin was now gray, thin black fissures fracturing across its surface. Onward Lumina walked, her feet making little crunching sounds as she stepped on the char and ash which had once been bluebells. The beeches that had sheltered them were now burned and blackened.

The sound led her to the hazel grove that lay just beyond. It had survived only slightly scorched, but in its center, not far from the cleft boulder, lay the old nanny goat. Her body was untouched by the fire, but the smoke had stolen her breath and thus her life. Meg sat next to her, weeping while she stroked the long floppy ears and tufted head.

"Oh, no..." Lumina moaned softly as she joined Meg by the still form.

A quiet rustle drew her attention to where figures emerged warily from the gloom just beyond the hazels. Fawns and does, weary from flight, made their way into the grove. Finally, Swift himself materialized out of the morning shadows, burned and battered. He moved with a hesitation that spoke more of pain than fear.

Lumina stood and went to her friend, placing a hand gently on his neck. It was then that she realized there was one missing, one very dear to her. A sinking dread filled her heart. She turned to look at Lorne who had followed her.

"Is the silver cat with you?" she asked, any quarrel she had with him, forgotten.

The widening of his eyes was answer enough.

"No," she said in soft denial. The knowledge that he might not have even been in the glade did not quell her rising panic. She raced away, back through the glade, calling out to him, Lorne chasing after her.

"Lumina!" he called, finally catching up one of her hands as she reached the edge of the meadow.

She spun around to face him. She had been warned that to kiss the Goblin King would bring with it ruin to all she cared for. And so it had. But the accusation died on her lips when she saw the devastation in his eyes. Though his deceit still gnawed at her, Lumina knew that he would not be one to secretly revel in her pain, with false sympathy on his lips. She could not say the same of the Fairy Queen.

She closed her eyes, the tears spilling over down her cheeks.

"Ah, beloved," said Lorne. Cupping her face, and gently brushing his thumbs across her skin to wipe away her tears. "What would you have me do to make this right? I would burn the world if you wished it! Wage a war the likes of which no realm has ever seen, if it would dry your tears."

His words kindled something deep in her belly. A molten anger that burned through her. To destroy that which had threatened all she cherished? That had taken from her that which she held most dear?

Oh yes... *yes*! The word trembled on her lips.

"Lumina! Lumina!" a watery voice called to her from the lake's shore.

She turned, the word unspoken, to see Serene and a very wet, very pathetic looking silver cat at the edge of the water.

"Dearest!" she cried as she raced towards him. Her anger vanished at the sight of the sad-looking cat who was trying desperately to get himself dry, but did not seem to know where to start.

"He was none too happy with me when I pulled him into the water," the nixy said, as she gently stroked the silver fur, drawing water out with each pass of her webbed hand. "He still isn't, I am afraid. But I had to! The fire was all but chasing him, or so it seemed, and I did not think it would be right for the fire to have him if my water could not. Besides, I didn't want my rose to die... and you did say that it would only bloom for as long as he lived. So, I took him and kept him safe until I heard your voice."

Lumina picked up the very unhappy cat and hugged him to her, and he let her, tucking his nose into her neck and purring despite his sodden state.

"Mistress, we owe you a debt," Lorne said from where he stood next to her. "Ask and if it is in my power to give it to you, I will."

"Really," said Serene, "anything in your power?" Her voice, usually child-like, had become shrewd. "Then I would ask this of you Goblin King, give me a door to the Goblin Market so that I may visit from time to time."

"Such a thing may bring trouble from the Fairy Queen," he pointed out.

"Oh, I think that after this tale ends, such a thing may be no trouble at all," she said coyly.

"Then after my wedding, if your foretelling is true, I will grant you a doorway to my city," Lorne promised, giving a slight bow to the nixy.

"Your promise made, Goblin King, I will tell you a little secret. I would not have thought a debt owed to me from Lumina, nor from the silver cat, but one would be a fool to turn down a favor from a king," said the nixy, her usual sweet smile once again lighting her face.

Turning to Lumina, she said. "And now my good sprite, clear the ashes out of your eyes and look with your heart which always sees the clearest." With that admonishment, the nixy stepped onto the back of a huge silver fish.

"Remember your promise," she said to Lorne, and waved as the fish dove into the depths of the lake.

Lumina turned, and without a word to the goblin standing next to her, walked back towards the glade. She understood what the nixy was telling her. She could feel life beneath her feet, the seeds nestled in the earth waiting for the spring rains. And though all was char and ash above the ground, the living roots remained below it. She could hear the voices of the pine and the beeches, even that of her wild rose. They would live. And when winter let go his grip on the world, they would once again open leaf and bud in the spring sun. Her steps became lighter, so that she almost floated until she reached the rowan tree.

"My birds are all gone," the Rowan Maiden said as she looked up at Lumina and Lorne, sap flowing like tears from her anguished eyes. "They flew away, but we could not. The fire burnt our skin so that it cracked and split. A single child is all I now have." Opening her hand to show Lumina the single berry that rested in her palm.

Hope blossomed in Lumina's heart. Reaching out, she covered the Rowan Maiden's hands with her own, cocooning the berry between them.

"One is all we need," she said, letting her hope shine

through her eyes. "Find a place for your child to grow, and I will make sure his roots grow deep and his branches strong."

They found a place nestled amongst his father's roots, a small patch of earth lit by the new morning sun. The Rowan Maiden tucked the berry into its bed of earth and Lumina smoothed the soil blanket over the top of it. All the while she sang, just as she had with old man apple in the eld woman's garden at the edge of the woods.

It was harder to breathe life into something when the world around her was preparing for winter's long sleep. More so, when so much of it had been destroyed. But, just as in the Queen's garden, the earth was not as barren as it appeared. By the time she was done, the Rowan Maiden was wrapped protectively around the slender trunk of a small tree. And Lumina, like a midwife after a long and difficult birth, was slumped over with exhaustion. But her heart was warm and full with the sense that all the world was right. She curled up there on the ground and fell into a deep sleep.

Lorne watched over Lumina as she slept. The silver cat, who had not left her side since they had found him, was curled up under her chin. Soot smudged them both, black streaks he wanted to wash away. He had also felt the power that had fed the fire. It was not a natural thing, and it made him wonder. Lumina's anger might have faded quickly, but his still burned bright. Truth be told, he was near incandescent with rage. Had she said yes, then much more than her poor glade would lay in ashes now. But she had not, and now he was left with a towering anger and no one onto whom he could turn his wrath, though he had his suspicions. But suspicions were not enough to wage a war that would leave the crystal throne cracked and the trees of Underhill piles of slag.

"Sire!" a chorus of sweet voices called. Lorne turned to see the circle of loireag he had set to weaving his bride's wedding dress hurrying towards him. They were carrying something.

"We saved it, sire," they said, proudly displaying the bundle they held in their hands. If the moon and stars had been woven into a fabric, it would look like the cloth they held so carefully.

Perhaps their obvious pride and happiness would have soothed his anger a little, if Hoax had not at that moment stepped out from the hazel grove carrying the body of the old nanny goat gently in his arms. Meg walked beside him, the soft sound of her lamentation filling the now still air.

Lorne watched as they carried her to the edge of the meadow where the clover grew sweetly in the summer. There, Hoax laid her down, and Meg placed her hands on the earth, asking it to take in the lifeless body. The nanny goat slowly sank into the soil's welcoming embrace.

"Ah, poor thing," said one of the weavers, shaking her head. "The mistress will be so sad. She holds everything here dear to her heart, and now look at it all."

"The Fairy Queen warned that all could come to ruin," said another shaking her head.

Lorne turned his attention back to the weavers.

"Did she now?" he said, ice replacing the fire burning in his heart. "When did she say this?"

"It was just after the Hunter's Moon. You and the mistress had danced through the glade that evening, before you took her across the stream to the Wood," said the first loireag, her brow furrowed in thought. "She came the next morning." The others nodded their heads in agreement.

"So, the morning of Samhain," he said. "And what did she say? Tell me as closely as you can."

"I am sorry sire, but we did not hear her ourselves," the third loireag said apologetically. "But one of our spinners was still on the mistress's dress when she was walking with the Fairy Queen. She told us that the Fairy Queen had given a warning, that all the mistress held dear would fall to ruin, should she ever kiss you."

"Which our fair mistress did, just yestereve," said Hoax, having joined them after discharging his sad duty.

Lorne closed his eyes. When he opened them next, all were gone, having fled before the tide of his anger. All save Hoax, who now stood at his side and his beloved with her silver cat, both of whom still slept at his feet. Even the Rowan Maiden had shrouded herself and her precious child in fear of drawing his eye. She needn't have. All that was dear to his lady was dear to him and he would never bring harm to it. Besides, his rage was not indiscriminate; there was a focus.

"There will be a reckoning," he said as softly as a lover's promise, and reality stuttered around them. "I will crack the doorway to Underhill wide open and lay waste to her realm. Call my knights and prepare my host. The Hunt will ride this night. They want to see a burning? I will give it to them."

Hoax gave him a small bow and a wicked smile.

"I am yours to command," he said. "However, I feel it important to point out, respectfully of course, that it is the eve of your wedding. And although I would revel in burning the Fairy Queen's court and crushing the floors of Underhill beneath my hooves, I doubt your bride would appreciate heads on spikes as wedding decorations. And I might feel it important to mention that the boy over which all this was started is still at said court."

Lorne's ire did not cool, but he could not deny that there was sense in his liege man's words.

"You see clearly, my friend. Clearer than myself."

"True, and what else am I good for but to show the blind what they cannot see?"

The morning wore on, and all the while Lorne kept vigil over his sleeping bride, his anger undiminished. Lumina did not stir. Finally, as the sun approached its zenith, the silver cat opened one eye and glowered up at Lorne.

"Don't you have a war to plan and a wedding to get ready for?" the silver cat asked from where he rested, still tucked beneath the sprite's chin. "Give my mistress some peace, Goblin King. No one will return while you stand there in a towering rage, and if they don't return then who will help my lady get dressed? Certainly not me."

So, Lorne returned to his keep to brood and plan and wonder what mischief the Fairy Queen was up to.

CHAPTER 15

Hollentide Eve

It was past midnight when Lumina finally woke. The sylphs had come through while she slept and scoured the glade, gathering up all the ash and carrying it away. The loireag had returned and laid out her wedding dress.

A few hours before dawn Lumina went down to the lake to bathe. Beneath the light of the sickle moon, she sat on a lilypad while Serene washed her hair and the silver cat looked on in horror.

Her own mind was awhirl with all that had happened in the past few days. It took very little thought for her to realize that the fire, which had destroyed so much and threatened to take even more, had been the Fairy Queen's doing. So though she did not know it, her thoughts mirrored those of the Goblin King as he sat in his keep, in wondering what move the Fairy Queen would next make. She had not seen her since giving her the key, a rash decision that she now regretted and was sure she would regret even more in the near future.

Lumina stood in the bright morning sun, just behind the screen of hazels, as Meg and the little weavers dressed her for her wedding. They caught up her hair with strands of pearls and ivory combs, leaving her neck and shoulders bare to the wind's caress. Her wedding dress was as light as thistledown and shimmered like seafoam. Over it all was a net of lace, its tatting a tangle of roses with jewels sparkling like dew on the leaves. If she were to look closely among the thorny canes she could see a host of creatures that took shelter there, ravens... stags... and little silver cats.

All the while, a merry group from both courts made ready. In the part of the meadow where the fire had not reached, and beneath the eaves of the Goblin Wood, low tables were laid out and filled to groaning with delights. Set along their edges were velvet cushions of the deepest hues, all in preparation for the guests who would attend.

When Lumina's attendants had finished with their efforts, she asked for a moment alone with her thoughts, and reluctantly they went. They had barely left when her hand was clasped by another. She looked down to find the boy standing at her elbow, resplendent in a coat of midnight blue and gold. He smiled at her and motioned for her to lean down. When she did, he gave her a kiss on her cheek and placed something in her hand. Looking down she found a beautiful golden seed gleaming in the palm of her hand.

"It is lovely," she said. "Is it for me?"

"Yes, child," said a voice from behind her... her own voice.

She turned and saw herself standing there. Midnight blue hair wrapped up in strands of pearls, amber gold eyes and a pointed chin. Even the dress was the same, opalescent white beneath roses of silver lace. There was one difference... a thin chain around her neck from which dangled a familiar key.

Lumina had no time to recover from her startlement before the Fairy Queen was standing right before her, kissing her lightly on the forehead, just as Lumina had done to Ember the day before. She felt herself diminish under no will of her own. Soon she had no eyes to see with, though she could still hear and knew when the Fairy Queen picked her up with her cool hand.

"I promised that you would be free of this and so you are," she said. "Had you not kissed him, I would have chosen a form in which you could still dance, a moth or a will-o-wisp perhaps. But you did not mind what I said, and I cannot forgive you that. Still, you will stay in this place with the things that you love. Come spring, you will sprout and grow, your roots sinking deep in the soil, and all will be as it should be. The king shall have his queen and the queen will have the key to his heart. Did you know that is what you gave to me, the key to his heart? After all, what is a queen's garden but the king's own heart, to nurture or neglect as she sees fit."

"Ah, sweet boy, there is no need for such sad eyes," the Fairy Queen said in Lumina's voice. Lumina felt herself fall from the Fairy Queen's cool palm to the boy's much warmer one. "Take this and plant it somewhere in the meadow. In the spring, we will come back to see how she has sprouted and bloomed."

Lumina knew when the Fairy Queen had left them and when the silver cat came to lean against the boy's leg.

The boy carried her out into the meadow, and made a soft bed for her in the earth. She felt the silver cat settle down atop where she lay, purring. She could feel his unhappiness and the boy's. She wanted to comfort them, hold them in her arms. She stretched and stretched; her toes dug deep in the earth, her arms breaking through the soil, reaching for the sun, and the silver cat took shelter under her branches.

She could feel the dry grasses all around her and knew she was in a part of the meadow not far from where the Goblin King would cross the stream to collect his bride. A part that was untouched by the flames from yesterday. She felt when Meg came to lead the boy away. Throughout the day she grew, so when the shadows of dusk began to gather, she could feel the night breeze dance through her leaves. On its back rode the salamanders; bright sparks that passed through her branches, they had come to cavort amongst the wedding guests or dance on the tips of candle wicks. But one stayed, to share his warmth and power. The sprays of blooms that covered her opened their petals to the gentle night.

She knew when the Fairy Queen had once again stepped foot in the glade and made her way to where she would wait for her King. And Lumina could not mistake the ache in her heart when the Goblin King joined her.

Ah, she had been such a fool! In trying not to lose all she loved, she had given it away. And there was nothing she could do about it, not even cry. But she could not stop herself from reaching for him, her petals carried by the wind in place of her tears.

Throughout the wood and across the meadow, fairy and goblin alike had gathered. Even the eld woman had come to see him wed his beloved lady. His love for her had banked the fires of his earlier anger, so that now at the time of his wedding his heart knew only joy. He crossed the stream on the feathered backs of his knights, to where his bride stood waiting, wedding cup in hand. She smiled at him as they stood together in the purples of the deepening twilight. He slid his hands over the top of hers where they clasped the wedding cup. She lifted it to her lips and drank. He in turn lifted it to his, the apple wine sliding across his tongue. In it, he could taste the sweetness of forever and the piquant bite of destiny.

"May you be by my side, from now until the end of time. Let our destinies be intertwined, your heart ever safe in my keeping," she said, her eyes aglow and her smile filled with happiness.

"My love will be eternal. My heart forever true to the one to whom it has been given," said Lorne, the promise filling his very being. The bitterness that had taken root in his heart so long ago was gone, washed away by the Lady of the Glade who had planted her seeds and made it grow again.

He leaned in for the sealing kiss, but bypassed her lips, sliding his cheek along hers so that he might whisper in her ear.

"But you were not the one to whom it was given," he said, and leaned back, lifting the chain with its key from over her head as he did so. "I know my own heart, Meave. But you never had one and so you cannot understand."

He walked past her into the meadow, to where a most unique rose grew. Its leaves were veined in gold and its flowers were the deepest blue. He had taken the wedding cup with him, and now he reached through the canes with it in hand to pour what was left at the rose's root. Gently he cupped one of the blooms and kissed the tips of its petals. The petals in his hand became a silken cheek, and his beloved's lips were against his. He smiled down at Lumina who stood in his arms smiling back up at him, the silver cat peering out from the hem of her wedding dress. The key which dangled from the hand that cupped her cheek dissolved away in a glitter of gold.

"It is not the queen's garden which is the king's heart, but the queen herself. You are mine and always have been and will always be, whether you wed me or not. Forgive me the grief I have caused you," he asked earnestly. "You are free from any debt that you may have once owed me, free to choose as you wish. So I ask you again, will you marry me?"

Reaching up, she framed his face with warm hands.

"Can you forgive me my betrayal?" she asked in return. "I was not a good caretaker for the precious thing you gifted to me. I gave it away and that was wrong, no matter the reasons."

"There was no betrayal. I gave it to you to do with it as you would, so there is nothing to forgive," he said. "Can you forgive me my deception? It was foolish and ill-conceived, but never done with ill intention."

"I am not sure if there is anything to forgive. You never lied to me, though you did not tell me all. And truth be told, I did not ask," she said. "But of one truth I am now sure, you love me and I love you, and what more needs there be. I will marry you, happily."

Reaching up, she kissed him, sealing their marriage.

The sweetness on her lips matched his own and he could feel that all was right in the world. He could also feel the debt owed for the wrong that had been done to his lady and the harm done to himself long ago. The prickle that shivered on his lips promised that whatever doom he pronounced would take hold, binding and absolute. He looked down into the eyes of his lady wife and knew that she shared in this understanding and trusted that his sentence would be just.

Together they turned to face the Fairy Queen who stood, as still as stone, at the edge of the stream where he had left her. Anger and sorrow filled her eyes, but Lorne knew them to be fleeting, just shadows and light that never went deeper than the surface. But he would change that now.

"You have done us great harm, Fairy Queen, without just cause," he said. "All in the name of something that you do not truly have, so I will give it to you. You are now burdened, Meave, from this day on to forever. Though you are still of faerie, and therefore immortal, a human heart now beats in your chest."

The words of Goblin King's judgment shivered through the air, and the Fairy Queen trembled beneath its weight. She fell to the ground and when next she stood it was as a white doe, her hide as pale as the moon. Her winter blue eyes were filled with anguish and pain. Lorne's heart softened.

"It is yours, always. You cannot outrun it," said Lorne. "In honor of the love I once held for you, I will not send my hunt to harry you and nip at your heels as you once did to me. For I truly hope that you find the love that you wished for, but never understood."

With a heart wrenching sound, the white hind leapt away, passing close to the boy as she went. He reached out to stroke her silvery flank and turned to watch her as she fled, his eyes clear but troubled. It gave hope to Lorne that perhaps the doom he had set on her would not be in vain.

CHAPTER 16

After All is Said and Done

The midnight hour had come and gone. And all but a few of the wedding guests had left to seek their own adventures. Lumina and Lorne sat comfortably on cushions that had been left for them, happy in each other's company. The silver cat lay curled up in Lumina's lap.

The eld woman sat across from them, the boy's head resting in her lap as he slept. Stretched out on her other side was Hoax, close enough that he practically lay in her lap as well. Not far from the phooka's feet and just to the other side of Lumina was a broad brazier with a glowing bed of coals where Ember now sat.

"His life will not be easy, standing between the two worlds as he does," said the eld woman, her hand stroking the boy's golden hair. "And I am an old woman. It has been a long time since I cared for a child. I hope I remember how."

"*Pfft*," the phooka scoffed, looking up from where he lay next to her. "You are not so old. And it has not been that long... a few centuries at most."

"Only you would say such a ridiculous thing," said the eld woman dismissively.

Lumina looked at her friend's face and saw the laughter in her eyes. She could not say if what Hoax said was ridiculous or not. She was not a good judge of mortal age.

"How old were you? When you left your village and went to live in the house at the wood's edge," asked Lumina, curious.

"It was so long ago, I am not sure that I remember," the eld woman admitted, her dark brows furrowed in thought. "Forty, perhaps, not yet fifty, surely. At that time, it was quite a venerable age, though certainly nothing compared to the age I am now."

"Which is nothing to the age I am, since mine even rivals Lorne's by a goodly amount," said Hoax grinning wickedly.

"As great as all that," said the eld woman. "Then perhaps I should not trouble you to carry us home. I am not sure such ancient bones could hold us."

Hoax was up in a thrice.

"Then allow me to disprove your theory," he said sweeping her a mocking bow, "and prove to you once again that such things mean nothing at all."

They begged leave of their king and queen. The phooka changed into a dark horse that shook its mane at the eld woman until she laughingly mounted on his back, the boy balanced in front of her. The silver cat woke up and decided to follow them, in hopes of a bowl of cream. He bussed his mistress's chin and headed off with them towards the eld woman's house.

As she watched them amble off into the darkness,

Lumina felt a scorching kiss on her cheek. And it was not the one that faced her husband. Turning, she found Ember's face leaning close to hers, though he was careful to stay away from the edges of her dress.

"I will beg your leave as well, my queen. Though if you have need, I am never far away," he said as he shrank, becoming a bright spark in the night sky. "Keep her well, fairy lord. She is a treasure beyond all others."

"Indeed she is," her husband said beside her.

"It seems we have been left on our own," Lumina said with a smile. "So much has come to an end. And yet, so many new beginnings have begun."

"Even as the sun sets every evening, only to rise again the next morn," he agreed, a mischievous twinkle in his eye. "There is one constant that you need never doubt. My love, my light, my sweet, sweet sprite... my glorious Lady of the Glade..."

She shook her head at his foolishness, but blushed all the same.

"I will happily play for you, an eternity if you wish it, if you will dance throughout that eternity beside me."

Lumina rose to her feet, drawing him up with her.

"Then let us spend tonight as we have so many others, as we will so for many more to come," she said, smiling up at him with all of eternity in her eyes.

The End

AUTHOR'S NOTE

The way some stories come together is truly a phenomenal thing. They can, at times, even seem to write themselves. That certainly proved true for *Lumina and the Goblin King*. It was a pleasure to write, and I sincerely hope you enjoyed reading Lumina's tale and about all those within it; if the silver cat made you smile even once, then I count the book a success.

That phenomenon can be true in our everyday lives as well; things that seem to happen by chance, coming together in unexpected ways. At least, that has been the case in my life, and there are a few people I would like to thank for that:

Celine, thank you for your encouragement, and your willingness to share your knowledge with me. Though I owe you the greatest thank you for introducing me to Kathy, who turned out to be all the things I had hoped to find in an editor.

Kathy, you are a gem! Thank you for your insights. I truly believe that the book turned out all the richer for them.

Lastly, I dedicate this book to the loves of my life, my husband Chris and my daughter Lena; you are my heart and my world.

And, to the small silver kitten I found by the side of the road.

GOBLINS, FAIRIES AND INSPIRATIONS...

The Good Folk in this book are drawn mostly from Irish and Scottish lore, with a good dose of my own imagination mixed in.

The Two Courts of Faerie

Many tales mention the two courts of Faerie. They are sometimes called the Seelie and the Unseelie, or occasionally the Summer Court and the Winter Court. Neither is wholly good nor wholly bad, though for humans, neither is wholly healthy.

There are two courts in Lumina's tale as well; however, I decided not to name them, and for a good reason. With names, come expectations and I didn't want to limit the story that way.

Of the two courts with which Lumina must contend, one owes its allegiance to the Goblin King; the other to the Fairy Queen, and never shall the two in friendship meet. The enmity between them is long standing, with good reason as you might have already learned.

The Fairy Queen's court resides Underhill where the crystal trees grow but cast no shadows. While the dark walls of the Goblin King's keep with its crimson banners and river of clouds, stands at the edge of the goblin's city. Though truthfully, they are both in the land of faerie, and as such do not bend to the laws of the mortal realm, but rather serve as a reflection of those who rule them.

The Goblin Host

Below is a list of some of the goblins you will meet throughout the book:

Bogels - a somewhat generic term for many types of goblins whose temperament varies from irksome to truly malicious.

Boomen - a hobgoblin of the Orkney and Shetland islands. Similar in nature to a Brownie (a common name for a house fairy).

Bodach - this goblin will creep down the chimney to pinch or poke naughty children while they sleep, filling their dreams with nightmares or stealing them from their beds entirely.

Henkies - short, squat trows (trolls) of the Orkney or Shetland islands. They love music and come out at night to dance around earthen mounds, called Henkie knowes. Henkies limp (or henk) as they dance, hence the name.

Glastigs - a water fae, she haunts lakes and rivers, luring men to dance with her before draining them of their blood. Her goat legs are hidden beneath a long flowing dress of green. She has another side, as fae often do, and is sometimes known to watch over cattle, and in turn, the children and elderly who look after the herds.

Powries - much like Red Caps, these goblins haunt old watch towers and the edges of ancient battlefields, wherever a great deal of blood has been spilled. They are murderous folk who take delight in rolling boulders down on unwary travelers.

Muilearteach - a blue-faced hag similar to the cailleach bheur who is born every Samhain bringing with her the dark months of winter.

Wulver - a man with a wolf's head found in the folklore of the Shetland islands. Benevolent, so most say. He might even share a fish or two with those who need.

Shellycoat - a water bogie who haunts the coasts and rivers of Scotland, so named because of the coat of shells he wears. He finds great fun in leading travelers astray, although he is most often considered to be mischievous rather than malevolent.

Cu Sith - Fairy dogs appear in the lore of many different lands, and each has its own name for them. How they look varies as well. Sometimes they are great white hounds with red ears. Sometimes they are seen as huge black dogs with glowing eyes. However, the Cu Sith of the Scottish highlands has to be one of the most interesting I have found. They are as large as a good-sized calf or small cow, with vermilion eyes and shaggy dark green coats. They can be harbingers of disaster and sometimes will foretell a man's doom.

Hogboon - A mound dweller of the Orkney Isles, this goblin can be helpful if shown the respect he feels is his due, or bring great misfortune if he is not.

Bucca - a Cornish hobgoblin that sometimes is said to inhabit tin mines and sometimes likened to a Brownie. However, they are also mentioned in association to storms and the sea. Fisherman will often leave offerings of fish on the shore in hopes of their good regard.

I haven't often run across them in my reading, but they are worth looking into further if you have the time.

Brownie - A household spirit often found in English and Scottish lore. They are very small, brown as a nut, and have no nose to speak of. Their clothes are often ragged, if they wear any at all. They help about the house and farm, often taking on the most tedious tasks. The only payment needed for all their hard work is a bowl of cream and a slice of bread or cake. However, their help can be easily lost if the work they do is criticized. And they may even undo all that had been done, adding more work to it besides if they feel the slight they were given warrants it.

Barguest - A bogie found in Northern England, it is often described as a great black dog bound in chains, with glowing eyes, huge claws, and on occasion, horns. It can sometimes appear as a headless man or woman. Which is the form I pictures when I was writing the scene where Lumina gets her first peak at the goblin's market, through the Mirror Gate.

Gruagach - Fair or haggard, male or female, clothed or naked, gruagachs have been described many different ways, but one thing they all have in common is their long hair. They would often help with work around the farm yard, such as minding cattle or threshing grain. Curiously, female gruagach have sometimes been associated to water, and will appear dripping wet even on the sunniest of days.

Loireag - Found in Scottish lore, this plain, diminutive fairy of the Hebrides is a patroness of spinning; and can be fiercely insistent that all rituals associated with such (spinning, warping, weaving and washing) be followed correctly. Loireag have sweet voices, often singing as they go about their tasks.

Bao Sith - Beautiful fairy women in Scottish lore who are said to have much in common with vampires and succubus. Seducing mortal men who are away from home to dance with them through the night. Only to disappear when the morning comes; leaving their victims to be found drained dry of blood. Much like glastigs, they often wear long flowing green dresses to hide their feet, which are in the shape of deer's hooves.

Piskies - Cornish fairies who tend to be older, shorter and more wizened looking than the British pixy. They enjoy mischief making, and take great delight in leading people astray. They have also been known to take horses out for wild rides late at night, galloping them around in circles called "gallitraps". They are not always troublesome and have been known to help those humans that are their favorites. They are most often seen dressed in red or green, clothes of those color being favored by the Good Folk.

Phookas - pooka, pwca, púca, pookha, phouka, pouke... so many names for a mischievous and delightfully tricksy shapeshifter. They are said to take on any number of different forms - hounds, hares, goats, even eagles - but the one of its favorites is that of a horse or pony. Usually a seemingly harmless creature who just so happens to be in the perfect place when a weary (or tipsy) traveler needs a ride. Of course, it is not the ride they expected, but a wild race over high hedges and through sucking bogs most often ending with the rider being tossed into some pond or puddle; the phooka laughing all the while. Sometimes the rider would come to a darker end, but usually the phooka is just out for a bit of mischief and is much less murderous than the Scottish Kelpie or Each-uisge. In fact, it can be said that they are generally well-disposed towards humans. However, they do enjoy leading them astray. Pouk-ledden it is called, and those that find themselves caught up in such a glamour can wander round and round the whole night through without knowing where they are. When the morning comes, they may find themselves far from home or standing on their very doorstep.

There are many places and times of year associated with the phooka. Samhain (Oct. 31st-Nov. 1st) is one of those times, which were usually marked when the last of the crops were brought in. It was (and sometimes still is) tradition to leave a small portion of the harvest, the "phooka's share", in the field to placate him.

I have to admit, I have always been fascinated by phookas even from when I was very young. A fairy that can be a horse? How could a little girl who loved horses not like such a creature! I still have a big soft spot for them, and they often appear in my stories, usually as irreverent rogues. They inevitably turn out to be some of my favorite characters to write.

Elementals

The four (sometimes five) elements have long played a part in ancient folklore and alchemy, and elementals were often seen as the embodiment of these elements.

Salamanders are often associated with fire in classical folklore. Usually, they are pictured very much the same as your regular, every-day salamanders, looking not much different than the one you might find in your backyard. However, in folklore they could not be harmed by fire and it was believed that they could even control or start fires. I took great liberties with them in the story. How could I not? It is so easy to see figures dancing in the flames and wonder how the fire would see the world beyond.

Sylphs are another such elemental. Invisible beings with an affinity for air, I pictured them as whimsical and easily distracted. It isn't too hard to imagine them riding on the winds as they race over the earth.

Nixies are not elementals, but they are water spirits generally found in Germanic folklore. There are a variety of names for them: neck, nicor, nokk, nix, nixy, nokken... just to name a few. They are said to be shapeshifters and are sometimes pictured as having a tail, much like mermaids, or having feet like a frog. When in her human form, a Nixy can often be recognized by the wet hem of her dress.

Truthfully, you will find spirits in many things as you explore myths and folklore. Trees, for example, have long been held as sacred. Elder, oak, thorn, and ash; willow, rowan, apple and hazel; each of these trees, and many more besides, are considered to be the haunts of fairies or to have spirits of their own. Each one comes with its own set of rules and warnings. The Rowan Maiden in Lumina's glade is just such a spirit, living in harmony with her rowan tree, and changing with the seasons as he does.

Tamlin

The story of Tam Lin is a centuries old ballad originating from the borderlands of Scotland. It tells of a mortal woman, Janet, who loses her heart to a handsome rogue named Tam Lin.

Janet was the strong-minded daughter of a lord, who when hearing of the fairy knight Tam Lin, vowed to meet him. Ignoring her father's warnings, she left his castle to go to Caterhaugh Woods where Tam Lin was said to be.

Beneath the shadow of the trees she found an old well where a fairy horse stood grazing. She picked a rose from the bush growing there, and soon the handsome Tam lin appeared.

Dismissing the cautions of her father, Janet had brought nothing material with her with which to pay the knight's toll, so she had no choice but to give him her heart as payment.

After returning home, it soon became clear she was with child. When asked who the father was, she proclaimed that her lover was no mortal knight, but the elfin knight, Tam Lin. In pride and shame she left her father's house, returning to Caterhaugh where she went to the old well, and plucked a rose, summoning Tam Lin.

When he appeared, she told him of their child, at which time he confessed that he was, in truth, a mortal man whom the queen of the faeries had stolen away. He feared the Fairy Queen planned to use his mortal soul to pay the tithe which she owed to hell. However, if Janet was willing, she could win him and save his soul from damnation.

Knowing now that he was mortal, Janet promised that she would do all she could. So, he told her of the trials which she would have to endure to save him.

The fairies tithe was paid every seven years, on Halloween, which happened to be that very night. Janet returned home long enough to put on her mantel and her gold ring, then made her way to the crossroads to wait for Tam Lin.

As the fairy host rode by, she hid in the shadow of a cross which stood there, biding her time until she saw her lover's milk-white horse. When it appeared, she ran to it and pulled the knight riding there down from its back. Janet held him tight as the Fairy Queen turned him into many fearsome and terrible things. She endured until she was left with only a burning coal in the palm of her hand, which she threw into the font at the foot of the cross. From its waters Tam Lin rose, naked and once again free of the Fairy Queen's power.

Enraged the queen cursed them and promised Tam Lin that had she known what was to come she would have plucked his eyes out long ago and given him ones made of wood (or stone depending on the telling) instead. Janet and Tam Lin went to Janet's father for his blessing and afterwards were wed.

The story of Tam Lin has many versions and has been made into numerous books and songs over the years. The one I referenced was sourced from *English and Scottish Popular Ballads*, 1882-1898 by Francis James Child. You will also find several variations of the names through-out the different stories; Janet, Janette, Magrit, Margaret, Tam Lin, Tamlane, Tamlin, Tomlin, to name a few.

There is so much more! If your interest is piqued or you just want to learn more about fairies, goblins and the like, then here are some resources that I have used that might go a ways to satisfying your curiosity:

The Encyclopedia of Celtic Mythology and Folklore by Patricia Monaghan

An Encyclopedia of Fairies: Hobgoblins, Brownies, Bogies, & Other Supernatural Creatures by Katharine Briggs

Encyclopedia of Fairies in World Folklore and Mythology by Theresa Bane

Faeries by Brian Froud and Alan Lee

Spirits, Fairies, Leprechauns, and Goblins – an encyclopedia by Carol Rose

www.ingramcontent.com/pod-product-compliance
Lightning Source LLC
Chambersburg PA
CBHW060810190726
48285CB00002B/613